AUDITION

Renaissance man for the modern age, **RYU MURAKAMI** has played drums for a rock group, made movies and hosted a TV talk show. His first novel, *Almost Transparent Blue*, written while he was still a student, was awarded Japan's most coveted literary prize and went on to sell over a million copies. He is also the author of *In the Miso Soup* and *Piercing*, both published in English by Bloomsbury.

AUDITION

RYU MURAKAMI

Translated by Ralph McCarthy

BLOOMSBURY
LONDON · NEW DELHI · NEW YORK · SYDNEY

First published in Great Britain 2009
This paperback edition published 2010

Copyright © 2009 by Ryu Murakami
Translation copyright © 2009 by Ralph McCarthy

The moral right of the author and translator has been asserted

Bloomsbury Publishing Plc,
50 Bedford Square,
London WC1B 3DP

Bloomsbury Publishing, London, New Delhi, New York, Sydney

www.bloomsbury.com

Bloomsbury is a trademark of Bloomsbury Publishing Plc

A CIP catalogue record for this book
is available from the British Library

ISBN 978 1 4088 0072 0

10 9

Typeset by Hewer Text UK Ltd, Edinburgh
Printed and bound in Great Britain by CPI (UK) Ltd, Croydon CR0 4YY

'WHY DON'T YOU FIND yourself a new wife, Pops?'

It was this question, posed by his son, Shige, that precipitated Aoyama's decision to remarry.

Shige's mother, Ryoko, had died of a viral cancer some seven years before, when he was eight and Aoyama thirty-five. Because of her relative youth, Ryoko's cancer had spread rapidly. She was operated on once, but recurrence was almost immediate, and within a month it was all over.

'She didn't have *time* to suffer, or even to grieve,' Aoyama had told a close friend at the time.

Ryoko's father was the owner of a venerable little firm that had been manufacturing fine musical instruments for generations. He and his wife, devotees of jazz and classical music, had raised their only daughter in a strict but loving household. Ryoko was cultured, intelligent and strikingly attractive. She was also a woman of great inner strength, and as a wife she'd been quietly supportive of Aoyama in every aspect of his life and career. He would never forget that it was only because of her help and understanding that he'd succeeded in his Great Adventure: leaving the giant ad agency where he'd worked for more than a decade to start his own video production company.

Although this was during the bubble years, when it seemed to be raining money, the sheer number of fledgling production companies ensured fierce competition, and for many months Aoyama's adventure had teetered on the brink of bankruptcy. Ryoko's father was the one who'd saved him. His firm had designed and built pipe organs for Catholic churches throughout South-East Asia, where VCRs were just beginning to proliferate, and Aoyama hit upon the idea of producing a simple visual presentation of scenes from the New Testament. Dubbed into the various languages, these videos sold literally hundreds of thousands of copies – thanks almost entirely to the old man's connections.

Many wives might have made a point of dangling something like that over their husbands' heads, but not the ever-modest and self-effacing Ryoko. Naturally, Aoyama had nothing but love, respect and gratitude for this remarkable wife of his, and yet it is also true that ever since his days at the agency he'd been rather extravagantly unfaithful to her. The most critical instance had occurred just after the Jesus video took off, when he got entangled with a nightclub hostess to the

2

tune of millions of yen. But even then Ryoko had maintained her cool and her quiet dignity, and no serious fights ever occurred in the home. Her main priorities – first, last and always – were Shige's well-being and education.

What husband has never speculated how free he might feel if his wife were suddenly out of the picture? And how many count the days till she takes the kids off for a week with her folks? Let these men actually lose their wives, however, and few can even summon the will or energy to run wild; it's only then that they recognise the support system they've been taking for granted. When Aoyama lost Ryoko he became mired in feelings of utter powerlessness. Eventually he'd consulted with a physician friend, who warned him he was just a step shy of clinical depression. 'You really will get ill if you don't set some positive goals for yourself,' this friend had said, and Aoyama set himself two.

One was to spend as much time as possible with his son. Shige was in a similar state of shock, devastated by his mother's death, and Aoyama conscientiously went about finding things the two of them could do together. He bought a baseball and gloves, honed his skill at video games and watched more movies than he had in years. But, because he'd always entrusted the business of raising the boy to Ryoko, it took weeks before he really felt they were getting to know each other. Swimming was one activity that provided them with a lot of quality time. Aoyama took out a membership at a local sports club and the two of them swam in the pool almost every evening. Shige had been intimidated by the water but his father patiently helped him overcome his fear, teaching him first breaststroke and then the crawl.

It was some six months after Ryoko's death, when Shige had got to the point where he could swim a hundred metres' crawl, that Aoyama realised they were both finally on the road to recovery. Ryoko had died in midwinter, and now it was the rainy season. Walking through the car park of the sports club, Shige pointed at a cluster of hydrangeas and said, 'Pretty, aren't they, Daddy?' They really were pretty, Aoyama thought. The vivid purple of the blossoms was something he could almost *feel* in the pleasant, after-swim fatigue of his body. It had been a long time since he or Shige had been able to appreciate things like flowers.

His second goal was to bring a certain legendary pipe organist to Japan. This elderly musician, who'd lived all her life in eastern Germany, was known to enthusiasts worldwide without ever having given a commercial recital. Aoyama launched his quest by carefully composing a long letter to her, researching the history of Christianity, the life of Bach and the culture of medieval Europe as he went. He had the letter translated into German, began studying the language himself and even started investigating possible venues for her to perform in. Promoters tended to laugh him out of the room the moment he mentioned the elderly virtuoso's name, but Aoyama was determined to succeed – and through his own efforts alone. He didn't enlist the help of Ryoko's father, or even let the old man know what he was up to. And when, after two years of sending letters without any indication that she was reading them, he finally received a reply – and although the reply was a simple, polite refusal to perform, Aoyama literally shed tears of joy. He continued writing to her, dozens of letters to the effect that it was our duty as Believers to record and commemorate, with state-of-the-art technology, her performance on an instrument of the finest quality. Aoyama didn't actually believe in God, but his experience with the Jesus video had served him well, and five years after he'd sent the first letter he was able to bring the legendary artist to Japan. She performed a free, one-time-only concert at the auditorium of a music school in Mejiro, and Aoyama recorded the event on both video and film. No one was more delighted about this triumph than Ryoko's father, who understood well what it symbolised to his son-in-law: a final requiem for Ryoko and the beginning of a new life.

At fifteen, Shige was already taller than Aoyama's 174 centimetres and a much faster swimmer of both the crawl and breaststroke. They'd both begun playing tennis the year after Ryoko's death, but of course Shige, who took after his mother in both looks and character, had made much quicker progress. The two of them stayed on in the house in Suginami-ku, a substantial home on an 800-square-metre lot that Aoyama rented from an acquaintance of Ryoko's father. The owner was an ancient gentleman who'd once composed popular songs and who now lived at the foot of Mount Fuji, in a retirement home with its own hot springs. The rent – roughly half a million yen a month – was easily affordable now that Aoyama's firm was well established. At his office, in a building on Meiji Boulevard in Shibuya, he employed a staff of fourteen.

Shige had entered a private high school in western Tokyo. He excelled at English and biology in particular, and he had a lot of friends. It was on a Sunday afternoon in midsummer, as the two of them sat in the living-room watching a women's marathon, that he posed the question that started it all.

The living-room took up most of the first floor. It contained a massive sectional sofa; a big, square coffee-table; a twenty-seven-inch TV; an audio rack; and a huge mahogany drinks cabinet. Aoyama was stretched out on the sofa, sipping at a can of beer. From where he lay he had a view of the garden beyond the sliding glass doors, framed by the lace curtains that

6

Ryoko had hemmed and hung so long ago. The housekeeper, Rie-san, was out there with Gangsta the beagle, who was barking and scampering in circles around her. Rie-san was forty-nine, a large, good-natured woman who loved *chansons* and travel and Furuta, the catcher for the Swallows. Aoyama had first hired her through an agency some four years ago, but because she lived near by and got along famously with Shige they'd ended up signing a long-term contract.

About twenty minutes into the women's marathon, Shige had come in, plopped down on the opposite sofa and said, 'What're you watching, Pops?'

Shige had begun calling him 'Pops' about six months ago. Aoyama sat up and reached for a cigarette.

'You're spending Sunday at home for once?' he said.

'I'm going out later on. Hot as hell out there right now. What's up with this?'

'What?'

'I didn't know you liked marathons.'

'I don't.'

'So?'

'It's women.'

'Not very pretty ones. They're all skin and bone.'

'I predict,' said Aoyama, 'that eventually women will outrun men in the marathon.'

'Because?'

'Physiology. Body-fat ratio, things like that. I'm hoping to witness the historic moment when a woman

7

becomes the world's fastest marathon runner. Guess it's not going to happen today, but . . .'

Shige shook his head and said, 'Somebody needs a life.'

'I've got a life. But a man needs to take a day off every now and then and just veg out. Rest the brain.'

'Any runners from Uzbekistan?' Shige said.

'Uzbekistan?'

'There's this girl I see on the train sometimes, about every other day? Really pretty. So I finally work up the nerve to talk to her, and it turns out she's from Uzbekistan. Working at a cake shop in Tachikawa while she goes to nursing school. Really, really pretty, you know? The girls in my school, it's not even funny how ugly they are. In middle school there were at least a few who were like, *Whoa*, but I don't know what happened to 'em. Where do all the pretty girls go?'

The cameras were trained on two Japanese runners in the front group. They were both plain-looking at best. Some years back, there'd been a Japanese marathon runner Aoyama had found attractive. He'd seen her in the Olympics. Was it Barcelona or Seoul?

'Beautiful women are like stag beetles,' he said. 'The all-but-extinct black panther, or that prehistoric fish they found off Madagascar, the coelacanth. It's not like you can find a stag beetle marching down the street, right? You have to go deep into the woods, under some tree.'

'Or to a pet shop.'

'They cost a fortune.'

'So where are all the beautiful women?'

'Well, there are swarms of them in the waiting rooms at Fuji TV, or in dimly lit basement clubs in Roppongi, but . . .' Aoyama stopped himself from adding, '*they* cost a fortune, too'. Shige had inherited from his mother a certain demure sense of propriety.

They watched the race in silence awhile. Aoyama found himself thinking how his perception of marathons had changed. As a kid watching Abebe Bikila at the Tokyo Olympics, he'd had a definite sense that the marathon was a symbol of something. It was easy to identify with the runners, with their dreams and aspirations. Back then, Japan as a nation aspired to something in which each individual seemed invested. And that 'something' wasn't just about economic growth, or transforming the yen into an international currency. It had more to do with accessing information. Information was indispensable, and not only as a means of obtaining necessities like food and clothing and medicine. Within two or three years of World War II's end, starvation had been basically eliminated in Japan, and yet the Japanese had continued slaving away as if their lives depended on it. Why? To create a more abundant life? If so, where was the abundance? Where were the luxurious living spaces? Eyesores dominated the scenery wherever you went, and people still crammed themselves into packed commuter trains each morning, submitting to conditions that would be fatal for any other mammal. Apparently what the Japanese wanted wasn't a better life, but more *things*. And things, of course, were a form of information. But as things became readily available and information began to flow smoothly, the original aspiration got lost in the shuffle. People were infected with the concept that happiness was something outside themselves, and a new and powerful form of loneliness was born. Mix loneliness with stress and enervation, and all sorts of madness can occur. Anxiety increases, and in order to obliterate the anxiety people turn to extreme sex, violence and even murder. Watching marathon runners on TV back in the day, you got the sense that everyone shared certain fundamental aspirations, but things were different now: it went without saying that each person was running for his or her own private reasons. For Japanese of Aoyama's generation, that might be a bitter pill to swallow, but . . .

Shige interrupted this train of thought.

'Why,' he said, 'don't you find yourself a new wife, Pops?'

Shige went to a friend's house that night, and Aoyama had dinner alone. Rie-san had left a pot of steamed rice, and he walked to a delicatessen near by, a place specialising in imported foods, and bought roast duck from France along with some smoked salmon and mushrooms. He wasn't particularly fond of cooking, but neither did he consider it a chore to prepare a meal for himself. He boiled the mushrooms and placed them on a Ginori plate, laid the salmon on top of them, sprinkled them with tinned capers, ground some fresh pepper on top, and added a squirt of lemon and a dash of soy sauce. There were more than a dozen different varieties of beer in the refrigerator – something that would have been unthinkable in the old days, Aoyama was thinking as he selected a Belgian brew and popped it open.

When he'd gone to meet the pipe organist, he'd spent three weeks in a little town called Wittenberg, in the former East Germany, about halfway between Leipzig and Berlin. Food and goods were scarce there, but it was on the River Elbe and the scenery was dumbfoundingly beautiful. Unlike bigger cities, the town had no food markets that catered to foreigners, and every morning he'd line up with the townsfolk to buy bread and to bargain with farmers for vegetables and meat and home-made beer. It was three weeks of an unwonted sort of monotony, devoid of any flash or dazzle whatsoever, and yet he'd never felt bored for a moment. Each afternoon at the same time he'd call on the elderly pipe organist, who lived in a simple stone house on top of a hill at the edge of town, and chat with her in his broken German about things that had nothing to do with the proposed concert. The rest of the time he'd walk stone-paved streets along the swollen, slow-moving Elbe or gather shell casings left behind by Russian soldiers in World War II, and every evening he made dinner for himself. The gas burner in the little house he rented was a relic, and just getting it lit was a major undertaking, but it produced a mysterious, pale-blue flame at which he never tired of gazing. Aoyama had experienced a real sense of fulfilment in those days. And that sense of fulfilment had truly changed him. The satisfaction he'd got from planning and realising the concert became the standard, the measure, for whatever he did from that point onwards in his life. Not even when making TV commercials or PR videos would he ever again settle for mediocrity.

Partially because of this meticulousness his business flourished, but the wildish lifestyle he'd maintained when Ryoko was healthy had lost all appeal for him. Which is not to say that he went without sex. There were always bars and clubs where one could find female companionship, and he had plenty of opportunities to meet women through his work; but he hadn't got involved in anything one could call an affair, or even a romance. At one point, friends and acquaintances had been all over him about remarrying. Even Ryoko's father had come to him one day, bearing a photo of an elegant-looking lady in her early thirties and saying, 'I know it's highly irregular for me of all people to suggest this . . .' But Aoyama declined all such offers, and eventually they tapered off. He came to be regarded as fiercely loyal to the memory of his wife, and though he didn't protest this assessment the truth was that he simply couldn't be bothered. He might have considered remarrying if he'd been too unattractive or too poor to get his sexual needs met, but that wasn't the case. The two goals he'd set for himself after Ryoko's death had taken more time and effort to accomplish than he'd ever imagined they might. He'd ultimately succeeded at both of them, solidifying his company's reputation and status into the bargain, but he had no desire to expend that sort of time and energy on a woman.

At least not until Shige asked the famous question, and added, 'You seem pretty down in the dumps lately. Seriously, Pops. What if you thought about getting married again?'

Yoshikawa, an old friend and colleague from the ad agency, had been doing TV work for something like twenty years but was now involved in film. Although their career paths had diverged, he and Aoyama still got together often. They had a certain deep-seated respect for each other, which precluded the semi-antagonistic back and forth that makes some friend-ships so tiresome.

That a talented man like Yoshikawa had moved from television to film was decidedly not because movies themselves had regained anything close to the power and influence they'd once wielded. It had more to do with advances in digital technology. Private, digital-based viewing systems demanded film-quality software. High-definition TVs were easily obtainable, but camera technology was lagging behind, and it wasn't financially feasible to make high-budget films solely for the ancillary markets. Negotiations with studios and backers were complex, and that was where a man with Yoshikawa's skill and experience was indispensable.

They usually met in the bar of some hotel or other. Yoshikawa had designated one in Akasaka for tonight, a fairly pretentious place with a lady playing a harp.

'What happened to all the real bars?' Yoshikawa said. He had arrived five minutes late and was tossing back a sherry on ice as he surveyed the room. 'The places where a couple of real men could relax over a real drink. Look around you – nothing but incomprehensible couples in this joint. Check out the pair slurping their Bloody Marys. Shit. They wouldn't recognise a really delicious Bloody Mary if they fell face-down in one. Ah well, let it go. But look at the two office girls baring their gums to the world as they yuck it up over whatever that is they're drinking. Gimlets?

I'm telling you, give it five more years and every bar in the country will have the atmosphere of a beer hall.'

'I don't know,' Aoyama said. 'I'm not one who tends to think bars were so much better in the old days. There was more discrimination back then, for starters, and that's never a good thing. And the belief that the cocktails in those snooty places were the gold standard is probably just another delusion.'

'Something's changed, though. Everything's all mixed up. And it's not only because the rich are poorer and the poor are richer.'

'It couldn't just be that we're getting older, could it?'

Yoshikawa thought about that for a moment.

'One thing I can say for sure,' he said. 'Everyone assumes that in ten years the world will be more or less the same as it is now, right? We all think, Well, I'll be ten years older, but we assume we'll be alive and carrying on as usual. In spite of the fact that an earthquake or an act of terrorism, or any number of other things, could wipe us out in the next heartbeat.'

'So?'

'So we act as if there's no hurry to get things right, or to do the things we want to do. And when I say "we" I mean everybody – from the average teenage punk agonising over whether to ask a girl for a date to the politician contemplating reforming the tax code. No reason it has to be right *now*.'

Aoyama had noticed that this doleful sort of tone was becoming increasingly common in his conversations with Yoshikawa. They were both in their early forties but sounded almost senior-citizenly at times. A few years ago they'd often joked about not understanding 'the kids nowadays', but this was different.

The conversation turned to music. Yoshikawa said he and his son, who was about Shige's age, listened to the Beatles together sometimes.

'You'd think that anyone who likes the Beatles would have no use for the crappy Japanese bands of today,' he said, 'but I guess that's not necessarily true.'

He told Aoyama about a video made by one of the younger members of his staff, documenting a female pop singer's concert at a stadium in some provincial city. Yoshikawa had happened to see parts of it, without sound, during a rough edit.

'At first, I swear to you, I thought it was a ceremony for some new religious cult. Tens of thousands of kids, all dressed and groomed exactly alike, packed into the stadium in orderly rows, all rising to their feet or screaming or bursting into tears at the same time. But none of them – not one – actually seemed to be enjoying themselves. They all had this look of blood-chilling loneliness about them, as if they were stranded on the dreariest planet in the universe. What the hell happened to those kids?'

16

As if on cue, the harpist began to play 'Eleanor Rigby'. 'Great song,' Yoshikawa muttered, and Aoyama nodded. The two of them listened in silence awhile. Aoyama had bought the single back in the day, and he tried to remember what had been on the B-side. He was thinking it must have been either 'Taxman' or 'Yellow Submarine' when Yoshikawa grinned at him and clapped him on the shoulder.

'So you're finally ready, eh?'

On the phone, Aoyama had mentioned the idea of getting married again.

'That's great,' Yoshikawa went on. 'Everyone's going to be glad to hear this. I might be a little pissed off if she's too young and beautiful, but . . . Tell me about her.'

'Haven't found her yet.'

Yoshikawa gave him a narrow look, then flagged a passing waitress and ordered another sherry, telling her to make it a double. There were four waitresses, all clad in long red velvet skirts, all young and all stunning. They were probably students working here part-time, which would make them twenty or twenty-one. Too young no matter how you looked at it, Aoyama thought as he watched those red velvet hips undulate towards the bar.

'You haven't found her yet? What are you talking about, then – an arranged marriage? Not that you couldn't find somebody nice that way, but—'

'Not *omiai*, no. Yoshikawa, you ever done *omiai*?'

'Hell no.'

'Me neither, but we know the drill. You meet the woman over dinner with the go-betweens, and then if you like each other you start dating. Which is fine, but once you've started dating it's not as if you can arrange an *omiai* with someone else, is it?'

Yoshikawa shrugged. 'You got me.'

'I'm pretty sure you're supposed to stick with one woman at a time. But who has time for that? I'm a busy man.'

'What sort of woman are you looking for? Younger, I suppose?'

'I'm not that particular about age, but nobody too young. Preferably someone who has a career and who's been trained in some discipline or other.'

'Discipline? You mean, like, bondage and shit?'

Aoyama laughed.

'Idiot. I'm talking about, you know, classical music, or ballet, something of that sort.'

'Ah. Shades of Ryoko?'

'Not necessarily. I just happen to think that nothing gives a person self-confidence like being classically trained. A person without self-confidence is incapable of being independent, and people who are dependent on their partners always create unhappiness. Always.'

'Aren't you being a little too picky?'

'You think?'

'A classical musician or a ballerina? I don't care how good a catch you are, that's asking a lot. You're not exactly Onassis, you know.'

'She doesn't have to be successful at it, or even a professional. Just someone who's seriously studied something.'

'So she could be an actress, or a popular singer, say?'

'I wouldn't want anyone who's been contaminated by the entertainment industry.'

'Can't blame you for that. It's an industry where people are bought and sold like cattle, after all. But you're setting the bar pretty high.'

'It would be nice to have a chance to really check her out before getting involved, too.'

'What, hire a detective?'

'Get serious. I mean talk to her, ask her a lot of questions about herself. Of course, the ideal situation would be to meet and interview as many different women as possible in a relatively short period of time. As for age, let's say from about mid-twenties to early thirties. I think if—'

'Wait a minute,' Yoshikawa said. He took a sip from his new glass of sherry, then leaned his chin on his fist, thinking. 'There's only one way,' he said finally and took another sip. 'Let's hold an audition.'

2

'TRUST ME ON THIS. Have I ever let you down? When it comes to holding auditions, I'm a pro, you know. Just leave the details to me.'

Yoshikawa got strangely fired up that night. Not content with quiet drinks in the hotel bar, he'd loaded Aoyama into a taxi and taken him to what he called his 'special place', a club in Roppongi. The hostesses here wore gauzy evening gowns, and the décor was in the Italian style, with leather sofas and etched, frosted-glass partitions separating the tables. Curious, temperamental-looking potted plants were strategically placed throughout the room, and inorganic Eurojazz played over the sound system. Though Aoyama knew that a place like this might be shockingly expensive, he couldn't see what was so unique about it. It was crowded, with men sitting even at the bar, but Yoshikawa was greeted by the staff as if he were some sort of celebrity. They were shown to an L-shaped sofa set in the corner by a waiter who was of a type one never used to see in upscale watering-holes like this: a dude in his late twenties with chiselled features, piercings in his ears and nose and lip, and a greenish-brown suit. He set a bottle of thirty-year-old Ballantine's on the round table, along with an ice bucket, a siphon of soda water and glasses, and expressed a hope that they wouldn't mind waiting ten or fifteen minutes. Meaning, of course, that all the hostesses were occupied at the moment.

'Definitely a nice, relaxed atmosphere,' Aoyama said when the waiter receded, 'and certainly posh enough. But what's so special, exactly?'

'Very simple. No bimbos. Ever since the bubble burst, the only women in the ruined clubs of Ginza are the sorts of nitwits who look like they just climbed down from the pole in some disco, right? It's like you were saying earlier: women who are serious about doing something with their lives avoid becoming airheads. The girls here are not only knock-outs, they're all trying to make it as singers or dancers or actors. Hostessing in a place like this is actually a relatively wholesome way for a struggling artiste to support herself. You'd be surprised how hard it is to pursue a career in the performing arts without ending up in porn or nude modelling. I mean, do you have any idea how many women are calling themselves actresses these days? It's an epidemic. Actresses everywhere you turn, and scarcely a face among them you

21

recognise. It's not as if we're making many more movies than we used to, but the number of actresses has increased about a thousandfold. Truly a bizarre phenomenon, if you ask me. But it's going to work to your advantage.'

He was referring again to the audition idea. Aoyama was no stranger to auditions, having supervised a number of them for TV commercials and PR videos. Sitting in a studio, sizing up a row of fifteen or twenty swimsuit-clad hopefuls, he'd always found words like 'slave trade' and 'auction block' popping into his mind. Of course they weren't slaves, but there was no denying that the women lined up on that little platform, posing in their bikinis, were trying to sell themselves. Buying and selling was the basis of all social intercourse, and the commodity an actor or model offered for sale was nothing less than her own being. Was it really all right, Aoyama wondered, to take advantage of such a system in searching for a wife?

'What's the matter?' Yoshikawa said. 'You're not even drinking. What, you don't like my sublime and brilliant idea?'

'I'm not saying I don't like it.' Aoyama lifted his glass and took a sip. 'I do have some reservations, though.'

'But it's the only conceivable way to meet your requirements! You worried about the money?'

'The money's one thing. What about the conflict of interest?'

Yoshikawa nodded.

'Point taken. But I'm not quite stupid enough to hold an audition just for you. That'd be fraud, after all.'

'Fraud?'

'Look. You could always take out an ad saying, "Wanted: second wife for successful 42-year-old widower". But do you think you'd then get to choose from dozens of lovely and talented young ladies?'

'No.'

'On the other hand, we can't audition women for some film we have no intention of making. That would be fraud by anyone's standards. What I'm thinking is, we come up with an actual movie project. A love story, naturally. We need a leading lady, and she has to be a new face, an unknown. Early twenties to early thirties, say. Only aspirants with a solid background in some sort of classical training need apply. That'll be an integral part of the story we come up with, that the protagonist is devoted to her art. So all your requirements are right there in the casting call.'

'We're actually going to make a film?'

'I didn't say that. There are dozens of film projects that fall through every year for lack of backers.'

'But doesn't that make it fraud after all?'

'Hell no. There's a big difference between holding an audition for a film you never intend to make and holding one for a properly proposed project for which you're actively trying to come up with investors and a leading lady and a script.'

'It's possible we will end up making a film, then?'

'The odds aren't good, but you never know with films. In fact, with films, your chances are actually better if you're just winging it.'

'Really?'

'No. But getting all tenacious never helps either. Until something changes about the entertainment industry in this country, things like tenacity and careful planning alone will never get a movie made.'

'So I'm going to marry the leading lady?'

'Why not?'

'Well . . . If it's a love story, that means that in the film she'll be involved with some actor. To be honest, I don't think that would sit well with me. Besides, if we actually do make a movie, the woman will become a real actress, and I have doubts about whether it's possible to lead a peaceful life with an actress. Maybe I'm just prejudiced, but they've always struck me as a fairly alien breed.'

'That's not just prejudice, it's the truth. There's no such thing as an actress with a stable personality. Show me one and I'll shave my head, stick a cucumber in my ass and walk on my hands along the Moruroa Atoll. So no, you're right. It would be a mistake to marry the one who lands the part. Besides, the odds are stacked against the film getting made anyway, so how would you explain it to her when the project disintegrates? How do you tell your bride-to-be, who's all excited about starring in a movie, that it's not going to happen after all? I don't care how strong her love might be, I guarantee you that'd be the end of it. Not the leading lady, no. Not even one of the finalists. What you want is a woman who survives the first rounds, the sifting of the résumés, one who doesn't seem cut out to be an actress but who's intriguing enough to call in for an interview. You may not realise it, but there are some real buried treasures out there. If we can get a little buzz going, so that a thousand or so women apply, we're bound to dig up a dozen or so of this type. The type 90 per cent of men will crane their necks to check out – but who've also got a lot more going for them than just looks. Some of these hidden gems have graduated from the very best schools, too. Not that you care about that, but I'm talking about genuinely intelligent women, proficient at classical ballet or piano or whatever, elegant and refined, nothing cheeky or affected about them. Women who make you think, you know – If only I were twenty years younger. Well, when I was twenty years younger I didn't have the money or status to get them anyway, but still. Women of the type I'd like to see my son marry, let's say.'

Oh great, Aoyama refrained from saying as Yoshi-kawa mixed himself another drink. *So we'll be duping only ladies of the highest quality*. But in spite of his reservations he couldn't help imagining himself surrounded by ten or twelve lovely, intelligent, refined young ladies. What man, if not homosexual or mentally ill, wouldn't take pleasure in a fantasy like that? The male imagination is a powerful thing, and it was enough to tip the balance. And to seal his fate. He had no way of knowing the unspeakable horrors that awaited him.

'Anyway,' Yoshikawa said, 'you probably want to hear more about how we'll arrange the audition itself, right?'

Aoyama nodded. He'd drunk half his glass of Scotch and soda and took a moment to look around the room. There weren't that many hostesses, but even in the dim light it was clear they were top of the line. Nothing gaudy about their make-up or clothing, and none of the Chanel suits that were the standard uniform of hostesses these days. Nor were the customers of the pre-bubble type – the big executives, or the realtors with their Armani threads and truck-driver crew cuts. These were men who looked to be in the music business or hi-tech fields. Money to burn, yet they were subdued – not because of any adherence to decorum and moderation, but simply because they didn't know how to enjoy themselves. The hostesses sat elegantly but attentively next to these quiet men, and Aoyama found himself focusing in on the former in a way he'd forgotten all about since Ryoko's death. The male stare.

'Depending on how you go about it,' Yoshikawa said, 'there's no end to the amount of money you can spend on an audition. Buying a full-page ad in the *Asahi Evening News* or *Pia* or *Tokyo Walker* can run into millions of yen right off the bat. And the really effective media of that sort are booked solid about six months in advance. So forget that. Newspapers and magazines are powerful tools, but they wouldn't really suit our needs anyway. How about the newer media, then, you ask, the internet or whatever? Well, that's no good either. You think the sort of woman a hundred out of a hundred men would want for their lover, or their bride, would have any interest in media popu-lated entirely by geeks with too much time on their hands?

'So . . . This may sound a little old-fashioned, but I'm thinking FM radio. Not the kid stuff – J Wave or whatever – but Tokyo FM 1. I'm pretty tight with an executive there named Yokota. He's an imbecile to the marrow of his bones, but he owes me big-time – he was once in danger of losing his job until I saved his ass by finding him a whole roster of sponsors. Radio's so much cheaper than TV, it's easy to sucker in thirty or forty sponsors just by telling them that FM is coming back bigger than ever. Advertising departments, as you know, are crawling with people whose frontal lobes are so underdeveloped that if you flatter them a bit they'll swear shit is platinum. I'll talk to Yokota, and we'll hijack one of the regular time slots to create a buzz about the audition. I've got connections with a lot of the production companies behind Yokota's programmes too, so assuming I bring along the sponsors there shouldn't be a problem. Believe me, Yokota isn't about to refuse if I ask him to devote a regular three-month programme to a theme like, you know, "Where is our leading lady?" How about *Tomorrow's Heroine* for the title? I'll have the copywriters in my office handle the script. Doesn't matter who directs it, anybody'll do, but the host of the show will have to be female. For the music interludes we'll use famous movie soundtracks. We'll choose a late-afternoon time slot, because you've got to get the students first, and you don't want women who are working regular jobs anyway. I mean, office girls? Forget about it. It's not that there aren't any beautiful office girls, but get a well-adjusted woman with a regular job and it's just not that easy to pull the wool over her eyes.

'Wait. I don't mean it like that. We're not going to be deceiving anyone. I'm just saying that the motivation for taking the bait, for buying into the dream, wouldn't be as strong for an office worker. Single girls living at home, that's our real target. The euphemism is "househelpers", but there aren't any who actually help out with the cooking and cleaning. The longest hours for them are in the afternoon. They're up and showered and have nothing to do. It's too early for a movie or a concert or a date, nothing decent on TV, so instead of playing with their own nipples and masturbating they start twiddling the switches and dials on the radio. The day's just starting for them, so they look for something light and calming. Why not listen to *Tomorrow's Heroine*? The lady personality hosting the show has a smoky, soothing voice. "What's more romantic than a rose still in bud?" she says. "Imagine for a moment. How do you suppose Audrey Hepburn spent her days before her acting debut? Or Vivien Leigh? Or Julia Roberts? They were just like you. Living each day unaware that soon they'd shine on the silver screen, and in the hearts of millions. That's right. They were all just being themselves, the people they were *before* they were heroines. And today, the heroines of tomorrow are also simply being themselves, living their lives, just like you. In fact, tomorrow's heroine just might *be* you!" '

Summer vacation was nearly over for Shige. It had been stiflingly hot in Tokyo this summer, and what with travelling with friends, a camping trip with the ski club from school and a long visit with Ryoko's parents, he hadn't been home much. Aoyama, for his part, had had several presentations for TV commercials just before and after the *o-bon* holidays, so it was late August before they had a chance to travel together, as they did almost every year, to the little hotel near Lake Yamanaka. Back when he was with the agency, Aoyama had once used this hotel as a setting for photoshoots featuring an imported whisky, and he'd liked the privacy and the quiet atmosphere of the place so much that he'd started making regular yearly visits.

He'd gone there with Ryoko alone at first. Later Shige had accompanied them as a babe in arms, as a toddler and as a little boy. And for the past seven years, during each of which Shige seemed to have grown at least a head taller, the two of them had continued the trips on their own.

The hotel was in a densely wooded area, about fifteen minutes by car from the lake. It wasn't particularly luxurious, the food was nothing to get excited about and regulars weren't given any special treatment. But the building, made of stone and wood and stucco, blended seamlessly into the surrounding woods; the two tennis courts were well maintained; and each of the rooms – of which there were fewer than twenty – was spacious and pleasant. Best of all was the privacy, and the fact that there was none of the forced interaction with other guests that you found in so many highland resorts and bed-and-breakfasts. Aoyama had countless memories of his days and nights here with Ryoko. They'd travelled a lot together in the period just before and after their marriage, but this was the only place they'd made a point of returning to every year. The car they'd taken the first time was a Bluebird 3S borrowed from a friend, and the late-summer drive down the Chuo Expressway to Lake Yamanaka was something they both enjoyed so much that it led to the purchase of their own first car, a used Audi they got with a thirty-month loan. From the used Audi they'd graduated to a new one, and then a Mercedes 190, although since Ryoko's death Aoyama had downgraded to plain domestic sedans.

The summer following Ryoko's death, Aoyama had decided, after some hesitation, to go ahead and spend a few days at the hotel with Shige. Shige was in third or fourth grade at the time. The manager of the hotel, a Schumann fanatic, was unaware that Ryoko had passed away. He came out to the driveway to greet them and opened the door of the passenger side only to find the seat empty. 'Will the missus be joining you afterwards?' he asked, and from the rear seat Shige, in an oddly sunny voice, said, 'Mama died.' The cries of cicadas and birds pierced the cool air, and Aoyama thought, *She'll never stand on the gravel of this parking lot again.* How many times had she climbed out of the car at this very spot, in how many different colours and styles of shoes, and said, as she always did, 'Up here you can really feel summer slipping away, can't you?' He had to face the fact that he would never hear her say those words again and never again see her slender feet tread this gravel. The death of someone close to you, he realised at that moment, was something you came to accept one concrete fact at a time. For four days, during which he and Shige played endless games of tennis, he worried whether an eight-year-old child was capable of such acceptance. They were both terrible at the game back then, which meant that they spent more time chasing balls than hitting them, but Shige never complained of boredom or asked if they could stop. Even he, at eight years old, seemed to realise there really wasn't anything else they could do.

Now Shige was fifteen.

'I hope Gangsta gets along all right with Rie-san,' he said from the passenger seat. It was a weekday in late August, and the westbound lanes on the Chuo Expressway were practically empty. The sky was clear and blue, and once they'd passed Lake Sagami they could see the profile of a snowless Mount Fuji. 'He doesn't seem to like her much, even though she's the one who feeds him every day.'

They'd bought Gangsta at a neighbourhood pet shop five years ago. Before that they'd had a dachshund, and when Ryoko was alive a Scottish terrier. Shige had chosen and named the beagle, but being a kid of shifting enthusiasms he soon relinquished to Rie-san the pleasure of feeding him twice a day, and Aoyama was the one who usually took the dog out for walks. But Shige still thought of Gangsta as his.

'What do you mean?' Aoyama said. 'They're always playing together in the yard.'

He was in a complex but elated mood. Yoshikawa had laid the groundwork for the audition with dazzling speed and an almost baffling fervour. He'd told Aoyama that the radio programme had been approved in no time. And now it was already on the air.

'My own team did all the planning,' Yoshikawa had said. 'The title is *Tomorrow's Heroine*, just like I said at first – what a laugh, eh?'

He had gone on to describe the female personality hosting the show as a thirty-something jazz singer just back from a long stint in the US, and said that the idea of disclosing the movie's storyline bit by bit had gone over big and the ratings were excellent.

'I thought I was indebting myself to Yokota, but the numbers are so good that *he* ended up thanking *me*. Most of the young guys on my team are movie fanatics, so the project has developed momentum all by itself. They're taking meetings with major distributors and potential investors every day, and the radio scripts are getting written without me even having to ask. It's taken on a life of its own – so much so that it's got to the point where people might wonder why you

33

should be at the audition. So here's my idea. Remember that documentary you were telling me about, that you did in collaboration with German TV a while ago? About a ballerina with a bad back and her wealthy patron, and an autistic boy, wasn't it? We could use that as the basis for our story, and then it would be perfectly natural for you to be one of the producers. Besides, it's a story with a lot of potential. In addition to finding the perfect bride for you, it's possible we could actually end up making a movie and pocketing a good chunk of change. Of course, if everything went *that* well, the gods would probably have to compensate by frying us all, but . . . Anyway, the programme's only aired three times so far, but get this: we've already received over two thousand applications. Two thousand women to choose your bride from. The wide age-range doesn't hurt, but, you know something? Maybe having an ulterior motive is the way to go when you want to get a film made.'

'Gangsta may not look it,' Shige said, 'but he's pretty delicate and sensitive. Kind of like, bashful. He doesn't warm up to just anybody. And Rie-san can be fairly rough around the edges, right? Like the way she's always breaking those expensive dishes Mum bought?'

'It's just three days. I'm sure they'll both survive.'

Before setting out, Shige had rented videos of ten or twelve war films and packed them, along with an eighteen-inch TV with a built-in VCR, in the trunk of the car. He was saying something about the Viet Cong now, but Aoyama wasn't doing a very good job of listening. All he could really think about were the two thousand applicants. Two thousand was a figure he couldn't even get his mind around, but it lent him a euphoric sense of unlimited possibility. How different this was from his mood that summer after Ryoko's death! All he'd been thinking as he made the drive that summer was that he mustn't let his eight-year-old son see him cry. Eventually even the deepest wounds can heal, and new possibilities can manifest all around you. It was an obvious truth, perhaps, but it struck him now as something profound and liberating. After checking in, he and Shige would play three sets of singles, take turns soaking in the big cypress bathtub, go out to the Chinese restaurant overlooking the lake, where the shark-fin soup and abalone were outstanding, then come back to watch *Hamburger Hill* or *Platoon* or *Rambo* . . . It was all very simple and healthy and gratifying.

'Not that I know that much about the Viet Cong,' Shige was saying. 'But were they really that strong?'

'In the jungle?' Aoyama said. 'Unbeatable.'

'Not even the Green Berets were any match for them, right? How about Spetsnaz?'

'Spetsnaz never fought the Viet Cong.'

'But I mean, if they did fight, Spetsnaz would probably lose too?'

'I don't think anybody could've defeated the Cong in their own jungle.'

'Incredible booby traps and things, right?'

'Mm. Shallow pits with sharpened bamboo poles planted under a layer of leaves. Smaller holes to shred your leg. Boards with spikes sticking out that would fly up and stab you in the chest.'

'And I heard they'd smear the spikes with poison, or with human poop.'

'Shit is free, after all, unlike bullets and helicopters.'

'Pretty scary. I bet they used the filthiest poop they could find, too. Get everyone to present a sample, and choose the one with the most bacteria and stuff.'

They were listening to middle-period Beatles as they drove. This was the result of a compromise: Aoyama would have preferred classical but Shige had lobbied for early Komuro Tetsuya. 'All You Need Is Love' had just ended. Aoyama looked at his watch, then turned off the CD player and tuned the radio to FM 1. A soft female voice purred out of the speakers, and Shige said, 'What's this? Why are we listening to the radio?'

Tomorrow's heroine. Where is she right now? Dreams really do come true, you know. All it takes is a little courage . . .

The first processing of the résumés would begin soon after they returned from Lake Yamanaka. *Two thousand women*, thought Aoyama . . .

36

3

THAT NIGHT, IN THE hotel room, they watched a triple bill of Rambo films. Midway through *First Blood*, Shige declared it a great movie, and he even shed a few tears at the ending. But with the second and third instalments he grew gradually disgruntled, and by the time they got to the final scene of *Rambo III* he was downright indignant.

'What the hell is this? It's ridiculous! How's a guy on horseback gonna take down an attack helicopter with a bow and arrow? They must think we're all morons watching this crap. What's he supposed to be, Genghis Khan?'

It was past two a.m. when the third film ended. Shige said he was going to get online and wanted the room to himself, because he couldn't relax with a computer illiterate looking over his shoulder.

'Go have a drink somewhere, why don't you?' he told his father.

Aoyama obediently left the room with a glass and a bottle of cognac. The hotel was utterly quiet, but lights were on in the lounge next to the lobby, a cozy space with comfortable sofas and reading lamps. He sat in the soft light, thinking about the audition and about Ryoko and enjoying the liquid heat of the cognac sliding down his throat. Ryoko's death, as he'd reflected many times before, had been a turning point for him. It certainly wasn't anything he'd hoped for, and he wasn't in any sense glad it had happened. But sometimes things happen that no one hopes for. Events that cause everything you've worked towards, the life you've carefully constructed piece by piece, to come tumbling down all around you. No one is to blame, but you're left with a wound you can't heal on your own and can't believe you'll ever learn to accept, so you struggle to escape the pain. Only time can heal wounds as deep as that – a lot of time – and all you can really do is place yourself in its hands and try to consider the passing of each day a victory. You tough it out moment by moment, hour by hour, and after some weeks or months you begin to see signs of recovery. Slowly the wound heals into a scar. But you can't expect children to understand that. For months after Ryoko's death, Shige had behaved as if he were on a sort of manic mission. He took lessons at two different tennis clubs, played video games and messed about on the computer all night long, and even began getting into fights at school, sometimes coming home with a bloodied face. It was as if he'd abandoned himself to his despair, but in fact, Aoyama knew, he was fervently searching for something. Something that, once found, would keep him from having to feel the pain of his wound. To just entrust oneself to time was to exterminate oneself, to temporarily accept a kind of death. Children aren't capable of that sort of detachment. For Shige it wasn't a question of whether he could find what he was searching for or not: the very act of searching served to create distance from the wound. Obviously Aoyama's own quest to bring the legendary pipe organist to Japan had served a similar purpose. If Ryoko's death hadn't occurred, he would never have undertaken the project. And if it weren't for that project, the person he was now would never have come into existence.

On the polished teak side-table was a copy of *Newsweek*, and he picked it up and leafed through the pages. It must have been left behind by some American guest, he thought; the manager here wasn't the sort to scatter foreign weeklies around for atmosphere. One of the photographs in the magazine caught his eye. A homeless youth in New York City. *At sixteen*, the caption read, *this boy has never been hugged*. Aoyama gazed for some time at the kid's face. It was the face of a human being who'd been constructed exclusively of wounds. Not time or history or ambition, nothing but wounds.

The face of a person who could probably kill someone without feeling anything whatsoever.

*... When my father's business failed, our family
moved from the big house we'd been living in to a
one-room apartment. He had a mountain of debt, but
I remember being very happy because now he was
spending a lot of time at home. At New Year's that
year, the streets were full of people dressed in their
finest, but we had no nice clothes to wear and our
room was dark and cold. We curled up in blankets and
watched a film on TV. It was an old comedy, the kind
that keeps you in stitches but then gets a little sad at
the end and makes you cry. So all of us – Mum and
Dad and my older brother and little sister and I –
laughed and cried and spent a really beautiful time
together. That experience meant so much to me that it
awakened a powerful desire: to one day become an
actress and appear in films ...*

'Kinda gets you right here, doesn't it?' Yoshikawa
said. Yoshikawa was now a section chief in marketing
at the mega-agency Aoyama had once worked for, and
they were in his office, facing each other across a
coffee-table stacked with résumés. 'Having them in-
clude a brief essay along with the résumé and photo
was a brilliant idea. The essay, amazingly enough,
gives you a clearer image of the person than even a

photo does. But just look at all the applications – we ended up with *four thousand*, my friend. On the table here are maybe a hundred of the most promising, and we'd like to narrow it down to about thirty today. Whichever ones strike your fancy, just slip them into this file. All right?'

There was a knock at the door. A young female employee came in with a cup of green tea for Aoyama. The office wasn't that large, but it was private. Opposite this sofa set was a big desk and a wall of glass that overlooked Ginza. Aoyama's eyes followed the young woman as she left the room. A photographer with whom he often worked had once said that when he reached forty he began to notice women's legs more than their faces or breasts. He'd also proposed a theory: that the legs of young Japanese women epitomised the best of the changes that had occurred in the decades since World War II. Aoyama was inclined to agree.

He gazed at the stack of résumés before him and sighed. There was no denying how discriminatory this process was. Out of four thousand applicants, the particulars on a mere one hundred stand-outs were piled on this table, while the résumés of the remaining three thousand nine hundred were packed away in cardboard boxes in the corner of the room. He now had to cull seventy from the hundred. *Cull*, he thought – what an unpleasant way to put it.

41

'We'll begin the interviews next Monday,' Yoshi-kawa said. 'It'll take at least a couple of days. I've got the conference room reserved, and I assume you'll be available?'

'Do you think we'll really end up making a movie?'

'I don't know. The script is done, but if what little I've read is any indication, it stinks. And we're not getting anywhere with the search for backers. In this country, as you know, getting a cast or director is of secondary importance – the only things that are abso-lutely essential are a script and money.'

Aoyama frowned. 'So it doesn't look good,' he said.

'Look, our main goal is to find you a wife, isn't it? Don't tell me you're starting to feel guilty. There's no going back now, pal. Anyway, what's so terrible about what we're doing? We're looking for your bride, your wife, the woman you're going to care for for the rest of your life. I mean, if you were just trying to find a mistress or whatever we might have to worry about divine retribution, but . . .'

Divine retribution. Aoyama repeated the words under his breath with a grim half-smile.

'Don't trust the photos, by the way,' Yoshikawa warned him. 'In a photo, even one that hasn't been doctored, the same woman can look stunningly beau-tiful or shockingly ugly. So if you get any sense at all that it's someone you'd like to meet, slide her into the file.'

42

Aoyama nodded and began sifting through the résumés. Judging by the photos, as he'd just been warned not to do, most of the girls were knock-outs, but he gave preference to those whose background included some sort of classical training. The essays covered a wide range of issues, though most of them said things like *I just feel I would make a good actress* or *I know I was born to act* or *I believe that acting would offer me the best means of expressing my talents* and ended with a plea to be given a chance. Aoyama couldn't fathom why so many of these girls would think they had an aptitude for something they'd never even tried. All it meant, surely, was that they were dissatisfied with their present circumstances. Rather than actually aspiring to the profession of acting, they simply wanted a new, more exciting life. It was impossible for him to imagine a woman like that as a life partner. Some of them were breathtakingly gorgeous, and many claimed to be accomplished at music or dance or foreign languages, but there had to be something wrong with any woman who dreamed of being an actress. Didn't there? In which case, maybe this whole idea had been ill-advised. Such were Aoyama's thoughts as, mechanically leafing through the résumés, he came across a photo that stopped him.

Name: Yamasaki Asami
Age: 24
Weight: ? kilos

Bust: 82 cm

Waist: 54 cm

Hips: 86 cm

Place of birth: Nakano ward, Tokyo

Employment history: Recently resigned after two years at a major trading company

Hobbies: Music and dance (twelve years of classical ballet)

Special talents: Dance, piano, baking

. . . After leaving the company I was thinking that maybe now was the time to pick up and head for Spain, where I've long dreamed of living. But then I happened to hear about this audition on the radio. I can't say I've ever thought I had a particular talent for acting, and I don't really expect my application to be taken seriously. But I was so drawn to the story that I felt almost compelled to respond. The story of a dancer whose career has been ended by a back injury . . . It so happens that I studied ballet for many years but had to stop when, at eighteen, I injured my hip. I don't suppose I really had what it takes to become a 'prima' in any case. But the injury occurred just as I was making preparations to enroll at a ballet school in London, and it felt like the end of the world. It took me years to recover from this disappointment. At the risk of sounding overly dramatic, it was a process not unlike learning to accept death. That's how powerfully the injury affected my life, and why I felt so much empathy for the main character . . .

Aoyama stopped to peer at Yamasaki Asami's photo a number of times as he read and reread the essay. It was just a snapshot, but her direct, up-from-under gaze was riveting. There was something powerful in those eyes, and her strong nose and sensuous lips made him think of Ryoko.

In the end, he selected thirty-one candidates for interviews, though Yamasaki Asami was the only one who really interested him. When he returned to his office that day, he told some of his staff about the audition, naturally omitting the bride-search angle. He explained that a friend and colleague from his agency days had asked permission to base a movie script on one of their documentaries.

'I myself might end up with a producer credit,' he told them, 'but at absolutely no risk to our firm. If the film does get made, however, we'll receive payment for the story idea, and I'll try to get video rights as well.'

He didn't expect anyone to object, and no one did.

Even as he was speaking with his staff, Yamasaki Asami was much in his thoughts, as she was when he returned home that evening and took Gangsta out for a walk. He could scarcely believe it himself, but he'd already decided that she was the one. The decisive factor wasn't her beauty, or the fire in her eyes, or her background in ballet, but rather those words in her essay: *it was a process not unlike learning to accept death.*

Being a beagle, Gangsta had one great passion in life: exploring smells. On their walks, he tended to spend more time sniffing at things than ambulating. Normally Aoyama would be tugging on the leash, urging the dog to move on, but tonight his head was full of Yamasaki Asami, and it was Gangsta who did most of the tugging. Aoyama was imagining an entire scenario . . .

Shige has eaten supper and is upstairs in his room, on the computer. Down in the living-room, where he sits sipping cognac, Aoyama can hear a faint tapping of the keyboard and soft electronic bleeps. Asami walks in from the kitchen, carrying a glass. She's finished washing the dishes, and now they have a chance to spend a little time relaxing together. She puts ice in her glass and sits down next to him on the sofa, smiling.

'I think I'll try a little bit of that,' she says. 'Is it all right to have it on ice? I suppose it's hopelessly gauche to drink such expensive brandy any way but straight?'

'Not at all. Good spirits are good no matter how you drink them. Mix it with cola and it would still be delicious.'

'I'm glad Shige seems to be accepting me. When I think about how I felt at fifteen, I know he must be going through a lot of conflicting emotions. But he doesn't even seem shy about calling me "Mum".'

'The truth is, he's the one who suggested I remarry.'

'You're teasing me.'

'No, it's true. You know, I'm pretty proud of that kid. For all he suffered as a child, he's maturing into an incredibly thoughtful and compassionate young man. Do you remember what you wrote in that essay, the part about learning to accept death? Well, all three of us have been through something very similar. Which I think is why you and I were able to understand each other so completely, right from the start.'

Asami nods and smiles and lifts the glass of cognac to her lips . . .

A yank on the leash brought Aoyama back to earth. They'd crossed paths with a female poodle, and Gangsta had made an aborted dash for her. Now he looked up at Aoyama as if to ask what in the world was wrong with him tonight. It wasn't until he noticed Gangsta goggling at him that Aoyama became aware of the goofy smile on his own face. Just thinking about Yamasaki Asami had caused the muscles to relax into a grin.

And yet he still knew nothing about her, really.

'Sorry,' Yoshikawa said to the girl he'd chosen to receive the applicants, 'but would you ask the next person to wait just a bit? We'll take a five-minute break.'

They were in a drab meeting room that Aoyama remembered well from his years at the agency. They'd begun at one p.m. and had already seen seven candidates. The interviews were scheduled at ten-minute intervals, but most of the candidates arrived somewhat ahead of time and were asked to sit in the corridor, where chairs had been placed, and wait for the girl to call them.

Yoshikawa, feeling that it was best to make things as stressful as possible for the applicants, had chosen 'the hottest young lady in Marketing Section Two' to act as receptionist. A male staff member worked the video and Polaroid cameras, and Yoshikawa and Aoyama conducted the interviews.

'Yokota wanted to be here, too, but I turned him down,' Yoshikawa had said earlier, as he handed Aoyama a printout of the time slots and names. 'I assumed you wouldn't want a third party joining us.' Aoyama had looked at the printout, but his eyes registered only the name Yamasaki Asami. She was number seventeen, scheduled for three-fifty p.m. His interest in the others was minimal, a fact which after seven interviews hadn't escaped Yoshikawa's notice.

'Aoyama, listen, you've got to ask some questions too. If only for appearances' sake.'

The applicants all bowed deeply before entering the room, and most were so nervous that you could see their fingertips – sometimes even their shoulders –

trembling. The receptionist led them to the chair facing their inquisitors, and again they bowed before sitting down. Yoshikawa's coldly businesslike manner towards them was probably intentional, and he varied the questions seemingly at whim.

Your name?
Age?
Height?
Ever worked in films or television before?
What do you like to do in your spare time?
Do you go to discos and clubs?
Seen any interesting movies lately?
Which actresses do you like, or would you like to emulate?
What would you do if you were handed ten million yen?
Who designed that dress?
What do you think is your best attribute?
Do you like Korean barbecue?
Can you smile for us?
May I ask you to stand up and walk across the room and back?
What if you got this role and your boyfriend was opposed to your taking it?
May I ask what your father does?
Do you like to read?
Who's your favourite novelist?

*Do you read a newspaper every day? Which section do
   you turn to first?*

What foreign country would you most like to visit?

Which do you like better, cats or dogs?

What type of man do you particularly dislike?

What sort of music do you listen to?

Do you like vintage rock?

Which do you prefer, the Eagles or the Stones?

Do you listen to classical music as well?

Do you know who the three tenors are?

*Which is your favourite, Carreras, Domingo or
   Pavarotti?*

Can you describe a vivid dream you've had recently?

Do you ever experience sleep paralysis?

Are you interested in UFOs?

Do you consider yourself beautiful?

*As a child, what did you want to be when you grew
   up?*

What are your views on marriage? And adultery?

What's the first thing you order at a sushi bar?

*Have you ever considered working in the sex industry?
   Or as a bar hostess?*

*Have you ever been tempted to experiment with
   drugs?*

'Why are you making me ask all the questions?'
Yoshikawa was saying. 'Don't tell me you've lost
interest now that we've reached the moment of truth.'

Yoshikawa seemed genuinely pissed off, and Aoyama decided it would be best to tell all. He asked the photographer to step outside for a moment so they could confer in private.

'Good lord,' Yoshikawa said with a wry chuckle after hearing about Yamasaki Asami. He found her résumé and essay and read through them, then peered at the photo.

'You can't tell anything from this, though,' he said. 'It's dangerous to base your decision on the application alone.'

'I know that. But I just have this feeling about her. Besides, all the others leave me flat. What can I do?'

'Intuition, eh? Is that what you're telling me? "Trust your intuition, and the universe will guide you"?'

'What's that?'

'An old saying, isn't it?'

'Whose old saying?'

'How should I know?' Yoshikawa sighed. 'Look, you need more information. You have to talk to the other women too, if only for comparison's sake. Isn't that what we're here for? I'll admit there's something strangely attractive about this Asami-chan of yours, but . . .'

His flippant use of the diminutive 'chan' was all it took to stir Aoyama's own anger.

'Yoshikawa, I think you know damn well how serious I am about this.'

'I'm serious too, you ass. So don't expect me to be thrilled that you've made up your mind on the basis of a photo and an essay.'

'You're the one who said the essays give you the best sense of who a person is. The written word doesn't lie. You can always tell if it's coming from the heart or not.'

Yoshikawa was silent for a moment.

'That's bullshit,' he said softly. 'But all right. I'll pay special attention to her too. Just please ask a few questions of the others as well. I called in a lot of favours to get that programme on the air – and even to secure this room.'

'Fair enough.'

The candidates represented a variety of types. One was a 28-year-old who'd graduated in French studies from a national university, spent three years in Paris as a member of a project team for a major trading company, become a clothing designer on her return to Japan, opened a boutique in Los Angeles and lived another three years in Malibu, then got bored with it all and began drawing illustrations for children's books. She was built like a fashion model and was wearing an outfit of woven hemp dyed in primary colours that she attributed to some Moroccan designer. She was also trained in classical ballet and said she felt that she alone was capable of undertaking such a 'sensitive and nuanced' role. Aoyama was sure there was no way he could keep up with a woman like this. Another applicant had appeared in over thirty 'adult' films, had twice tried to commit suicide, had been institutionalised three times and was now, at thirty-three, a yoga instructor. She showed them the scars on her left wrist as if displaying her most valued treasure. Several of the women came with their managers in tow. One of the managers literally got down on his hands and knees, prostrating himself. 'Please favour us with your consideration!' he screeched, as if begging for his life. One of the women claimed to be psychic and offered to describe the guardian spirits attached to both of them: Aoyama's turned out to be a painter who'd died young, and Yoshikawa's was a flying squirrel. A number of the women insisted on dancing for them, and one began shedding clothes as she did so. Aoyama wanted to stop her, but Yoshikawa overruled. She ended up completely nude, right there in the drab meeting room, and left saying she felt like a new woman. A girl still in her teens spoke at great length about her tumultuous sexual history. There were several women in their thirties. One had taken an aeroplane all the way from Hokkaido just for this audition, and proudly told them that she was known as the Queen of the Discos in Sapporo. 'Men have made a fuss over me ever since I was a little girl,' she said, 'so it seems only natural to have them flocking around me at discos, but I make a point of never giving my heart – or my body – to anyone. When people ask why that is, I tell them it's because I'm an actress. Not that I've ever done any actual acting *per se*, but I know in my heart that I was born to be a star.' One explained that she was eager to start an acting career because her husband had caught her cheating and was threatening divorce. Another, who'd shrugged off her trench coat to sit before them in a string bikini and high heels, said she'd appeared nude in a number of magazines but never got a true sense of fulfilment from that and realised when she heard about the audition that destiny was calling. A few brought portable karaoke sets and sang for them. They saw a nurse, a poet and a vocalist in a band, a woman with a seventy-year-old sugar daddy, a nursery-school teacher, a very tall African-Japanese, a baton-twirler and a rhythmic gymnast.

And then, at exactly three-fifty p.m., she made her appearance.

4

'NEXT, PLEASE,' CAME THE voice of the hottest girl in
Section Two, and Yamasaki Asami materialised in the
doorway.

Silhouetted against the off-white walls, she walked
to the chair, bowed with modest grace and sat down.
That was all, but Aoyama had a very distinct sensation
that something extraordinary was happening all
around him. It was like being the millionth visitor
to an amusement park, suddenly bathed in spotlights
and a rain of balloons and surrounded with micro-
phones and flashing cameras. As if Luck, normally
dispersed in billions of tiny, free-floating, gemlike
particles, had suddenly coalesced in a single beatific
vision – a vision that changed everything, for ever. He
was aware of an indescribable, fizzy sort of feeling in
the pit of his stomach, and of the voice of Reason in his
own head chanting the refrain: *This can't be right, it
doesn't make sense, things like this aren't supposed to
happen.* But the voice grew weaker as the fizziness

seeped into his bloodstream and spread through his system.

She was even more beautiful than her snapshot had led him to believe. And when she smiled as if to herself and shyly looked down at the floor, all his worries seemed to dissolve and leave him afloat in a warm bubble of bliss. He felt like a deaf man whose ears had been healed with exquisite music, and it almost struck him as odd that music *didn't* begin playing: in a movie, this was where the poignant love theme would have swelled. He glanced at the hottest young lady in Section Two and wondered how she was managing to maintain her composure. Faced with such beauty, she should have swooned with shame and slumped to the floor.

Yoshikawa began the questioning.

'You're, let's see, Yamasaki Asami-san?'

'Yes. Yamasaki Asami.'

What a voice, thought Aoyama, and Yoshikawa must have had a similar reaction, judging by the glance he shot him. It was a voice that poured into your ears and oozed down the nerves to the nape of your neck – neither high-pitched nor deep or husky, but round and smooth and crystalline.

'You heard about the audition on the radio?'

Even Yoshikawa seemed a bit nervous as he spoke.

'Yes, that's right.'

Aoyama was more or less face to face with her. Her semi-long, lustrous hair was tied back in a casual way.

She obviously hadn't fussed over it, but neither was there anything even remotely untidy about her appearance. Her features weren't exaggerated or dramatic, but every expression they assumed made a strong, clear impression. Aoyama thought it was as if her soul, or her spirit, or whatever one wanted to call it, lay just below the surface of her skin.

Yoshikawa asked if she'd ever worked in television or films, and she shook her head, no.

'There's been talk a few times, but nothing ever came of it.'

'Why do you suppose that is?'

'I think the fact that I'm not with an agency . . .'

'So you don't have an agent?'

'No, I don't.'

'Any reason?'

'Well, once – it was quite a while ago now, when I was still in college – I was . . . scouted? Isn't that what they call it? Someone stopped me on the street. I suppose I'm to blame for blithely going along with him, but it turned out to be a talent agency for porn actors. The whole experience was so unpleasant that I guess I developed a bias against agencies in general.'

'So you're completely on your own?'

'I do have a mentor who works for a record company, but I haven't been in touch with him for some time now.'

'Which record company?'

'Victor.'

'May I ask his name?'

'Shibata-san. He's a producer in the domestic music division.'

'Thank you. So. You graduated from college and went to work for a trading company. Now that you've resigned from the company, may I ask how you're supporting yourself? Do you have a part-time job of some sort?'

'I help out at a friend's place three times a week.'

'A restaurant or something?'

'It's a little neighbourhood bar, a tiny place with just one small counter. The mama-san is a lady I met a long time ago, at voice-training classes.'

'Do you like to drink?'

'Only moderately. Socially.'

'And is three nights a week enough to get by?'

'I also do some modelling now and then.'

'Modelling.'

'I have a friend who's a stylist, and she helps me get work occasionally. Not for major magazines, of course, but catalogues and newspaper ads and so on.'

'I see. And you live in Suginami? "Casa Prima" – I guess that's an apartment complex of some sort? You know, people like myself and Aoyama here, we don't really have much of a window on to the lifestyles of young ladies today. Please feel free not to answer this if it's too personal, but I wonder how much monthly income someone like yourself requires. A lot of young women seem to be living so extravagantly these days – carrying designer bags that cost tens of thousands of yen, for example – and I can't help but wonder how they manage that.'

Yoshikawa looked at Aoyama as if to say, *I'm asking this for your benefit, you know.*

'To be honest,' she said, 'it's a mystery to me, too.'

She spoke clearly and unfalteringly, looking at each of them in turn, and she didn't stretch out the vowels at the ends of words like so many young women, or fill her sentences with meaningless inter-jections. Aoyama could tell she was a little nervous, though he couldn't have said how he knew that. Somehow he just felt completely in tune with her feelings.

'However,' she said, 'I don't like to say it, but I suppose a lot of those girls, the ones with the incred-ibly expensive bags and jewellery and so on, are probably working in the sex industry. As for myself, I have a studio apartment, and the rent's only a little over seventy thousand yen. I don't go out that much, and I don't have any expensive hobbies or tastes, so a hundred and fifty thousand a month . . . might be a little tight, but two hundred thousand or so is enough to pay the bills and buy the books and CDs and things I want.'

Aoyama piped up for the first time.

'Can you give me an example,' he said, 'of what you mean by "expensive hobbies or tastes"?'

His voice was quavering a bit, and he immediately worried that the question was impossibly inane. But she smiled, and that was all it took to erase his anxiety.

'For example,' she said, 'I have a friend who raises tropical fish. She took out a loan to buy this huge aquarium, and now she's working two jobs just to pay off the loan. And another girl I know was collecting these beautiful wineglasses from Europe. She did word-processing at home and took on so much extra work that she barely had time to sleep and finally made herself ill.'

Aoyama could relate to this. It was something he himself had often thought about. In the old days, things like tropical fish or imported wineglasses weren't within reach for the average person. Now when you walked down the street you passed shop windows full of the finest quality goods from around the world. Any of these things could be yours if you were willing to sacrifice a little, and many people ended up sacrificing a lot. It's difficult to control the desire to accumulate things.

But it didn't really matter what she was saying. Aoyama was happy just savouring the sound of her voice. It was a voice that felt like delicate fingers, or a moist tongue, tickling his skin.

Yoshikawa continued the questioning.

'What kinds of books do you read?'

'Foreign mysteries, mostly. Not any particular author, but . . . I haven't done much travelling myself, so I love reading about foreign towns and cities. In mysteries and spy novels, you get very detailed descriptions of the streets and the buildings and so on, and I really enjoy that sort of thing.'

'Which country would you most like to visit?'

'I've never actually been anywhere except Hawaii, and Honolulu isn't exactly the most exotic place, is it? Morocco, Turkey, one of the smaller countries in Europe . . . Anywhere would be wonderful, really.'

When she uttered the names Morocco and Turkey, Yamasaki Asami tilted her head back slightly and a faraway look came into her eyes. Aoyama caught himself imagining the two of them walking down the stone-paved streets of that nostalgic little town in Germany. It would be spring or early summer. A riot of little flowers blooming beneath the eaves of the houses. They hear the songs of skylarks above them as they stroll arm in arm over the ancient paving stones and gaze at the soft sunlight that glitters on the rolling surface of the river. *Yes, I lived here for several months, did virtually nothing but go to church and visit that pipe organist at her home, and went to bed early every night. It was very monotonous, the same routine every day, but I remember it as a really special time in my life. I don't know, this may sound affected, but the beauty and silence of the place filled me with a sort of sublime loneliness. That's when I realised something. In Japan, even when you're alone, you're never really that lonely. But the loneliness you feel living among people with differently coloured skin and eyes, whose language you don't even speak very well – that sort of loneliness is something you feel down to the marrow of your bones. I always thought that someday I'd come back here with someone I loved, and I'd walk along with my arm around her, just like this, and tell her what it was like being here alone. Of course, I never thought it would turn out this perfectly. This is a dream come true for me, it really is . . .*

He couldn't believe how sweet this sudden vision tasted. His heart was pounding, and he silently took a few deep breaths to calm himself down. He'd better ask another question, he thought, or he might just sit there mooning at her, losing himself in daydreams. Besides, he wanted to raise certain core issues that Yoshikawa might not touch upon.

'You,' he croaked, and cleared his throat. 'Excuse me. You wrote that you were thinking about going to Spain after leaving the company.'

'Yes.'

'Are you planning to live there long-term?'

'I have a friend in Madrid, an old friend from ballet school, so it did occur to me to move there. But I haven't made any actual preparations or anything, which makes me wonder how serious I really am about it all.'

She lowered her gaze in a melancholy way. Aoyama studied this heart-piercing expression and swallowed.

'May I ask,' he said, 'about your experience with ballet?'

'Of course.' She looked up again and met his gaze.

'You said you injured yourself.'

'That's right.'

'It must have been awfully difficult to give up on something you'd devoted yourself to for so long. Of course, if you'd rather not talk about it . . .'

'No, it's fine. I can discuss it fairly objectively now . . . I think.'

She shot him a lonesome little smile as she spoke these last two words, and again he felt something pierce his heart. It was a smile of resignation, and he recognised it all too well.

'Stop me if this is too personal,' he said, 'but in your essay, I believe you wrote that being suddenly deprived of the thing that's most important to you is in a sense like learning to accept death.'

'I suppose I did write that.'

She peered at Aoyama inquisitively, wondering, no doubt, where he was going with this, but . . . *What a look*, he thought. He imagined her peering at him like that up close, in private, and whispering something intense. He'd probably melt into a puddle.

'It moved me,' he said, and she opened her eyes wide and quietly gasped.

'Ha?'

'I could relate to it. I think almost everyone has had, to one degree or another, a similar experience. Something falls apart on you, or is torn away from you, something that can never be fixed or replaced. You struggle with it and agonise over it and kick and scream, but there's really nothing you can do. In order to keep on living, you have to learn to accept the reality, accept the loss or the injury, and the wound it leaves. To be frank, I was quite taken aback to see a young woman like yourself selecting such a precise metaphor to describe that sort of acceptance and resignation. When I read it I thought, here's a person who's really living her life in earnest.'

Yoshikawa poked Aoyama's thigh with his thumb. Meaning, Aoyama assumed, something like 'Listen to you.' Yamasaki Asami took a deep breath and slowly let it out.

'I really did suffer a lot,' she said, 'and for a lot longer than I even care to remember. I was sure I'd never find anything to take the place of ballet, and it took all my energy just to get through each day. My parents and my friends all said that time alone would heal the wound, and I guess I knew that was true, but I wished I could hibernate or something, and let time go by without having to suffer through it. But of course the clock just kept slowly ticking away. *Tick, tick, tick* – like it was chipping away at me, at my life. Trying to do other things was painful, but just sitting around and doing nothing was even worse. I don't know if it's about resignation so much as . . . Well, death is the worst thing that can happen to you, isn't it? So in that sense, I thought it was like accepting death.'

'What do you think?' Aoyama said after she'd left the meeting room and Yoshikawa had sent the photographer out again and told the receptionist they'd take a fifteen-minute break.

'What do I think?' Yoshikawa said, reaching in his pocket and pulling out a new pack of Lark Milds. He took his time opening the packet, extracting a cigarette, and lighting it. 'I'm not sure how to answer that,' he said. 'There's definitely something about her that puts a man on edge. I can't remember the last time just talking to a woman made me want a cigarette.' He looked at Aoyama and sighed, emitting a stream of smoke. 'You're gone, aren't you. I mean, "Here's a person who's living her life in earnest"? Where'd that come from? It's not something you'd normally say during an audition, that's for sure. I nearly fell off my chair.'

Aoyama protested that he was only saying what he really felt. He couldn't remember, he said, the last time anyone had made that sort of impression on him.

'Well, there's no denying that she seems earnest,' Yoshikawa said. 'But something about her bothers me.'

'Oh?'

'Yeah. I can't put my finger on it, but . . . Well. Anyway.'

The rest of the auditions were lacklustre. Yoshikawa was tired, not to mention irritated with Aoyama for being so obviously bored and distracted, and he burned his way through the entire packet of Larks. Aoyama, for his part, had only one thing on his mind: how to go about meeting Yamasaki Asami alone next time.

He returned home an hour earlier than usual. He had the eight-millimetre videotape of her audition and was eager to watch it alone. Rie-san was in the kitchen making dinner and probably wouldn't leave until Shige got home from school. It was six p.m. now, and since entering high school Shige generally got home at about seven. As soon as he arrived he'd demolish his dinner in the manner popularised by starving lions, and then disappear into his room. Aoyama would have to wait until then to study the tape.

Once things had progressed a bit, assuming all went well, he'd show the tape to Shige, and of course he'd have to introduce her to him at some point.

'Shige-chan's kind of late, isn't he?' Rie-san said, turning from the potatoes she was slicing. 'It gets dark by five-thirty these days! Shouldn't he try to get home a little earlier?'

Aoyama was at the dining-table, reading the evening paper. Over the years, Ryoko had gradually made improvements on this kitchen of theirs, turning it into a highly functional and invitingly cosy space. During the day it was a better place to relax than even the living-room. The door leading out to the garden was mostly glass, and the big, south-facing windows made this the sunniest room in the house.

'He's all right. A kid has a lot to do at that age – hanging out with his friends and whatnot.'

'But there've been so many muggings and things lately! When I walk home at night, I'm very careful to stick to the streets that are well lit, believe me! If you cross through the park, where the light isn't so good, you see these kids – teenagers – loitering around in big groups, and, I'll tell you, it's very frightening!'

'Don't worry. I've schooled him in the ancient art of running like hell if he ever feels threatened. He knows what he's doing.'

'I know he knows what he's doing, but they say you can buy anything out there nowadays, even pistols from Russia or China! It's terrifying!'

'I've talked to him about that too. Rie-san, a boy Shige's age, if he meets a cute girl on the train, for example, he'll think nothing of spending an hour the next day waiting to see if she shows up on the platform again.'

'As long as it's something fun and innocent like that, fine, but . . .'

Rie-san was preparing a creamy stew. She made a lot of stews and soups for them, dishes that could be reheated and eaten right away. Occasionally Aoyama cooked dinner himself, but he made a point of sharing the evening meal with Shige whenever possible. Gangsta was right outside the glass door, and each time Rie-san walked from the counter to the refrigerator he'd bark: *Give me food!*

Aoyama imagined Gangsta barking at Yamasaki Asami as she prepared dinner in this kitchen. He even pictured the design and colour of the apron she'd be wearing. Gangsta would be wary of her at first, as he always was with strangers. But after two or three months his bark would change from one of distrust to one like this, imploring her to feed him. Compared to these seven long years, three months was no time at all . . .

Shige got home a little after seven and reported, to no one's surprise, that he was dying of hunger. Watching the news and wondering aloud how Japanese politicians had managed to sink to such depths of depravity, he polished off four bowls of stew, then he retreated to his room, saying he wanted to try out some new software he'd borrowed from a friend.

Now was Aoyama's chance to review Yamasaki Asami's audition video, but he remembered something even more important. He had to arrange to meet with her alone, and the sooner the better. He wondered if he should just call her and tell her the truth, that he thought he was in love with her. Yoshikawa would surely advise against it. Of course he wouldn't reveal the true purpose behind the audition, but why not candidly confess how he'd felt when reading her essay and speaking with her at the interview? However dubious the circumstances, there was no denying the impact that meeting her had had on him.

His heartbeat began to race. He had her telephone number. It was just past eight o'clock, so he probably had an hour or so before it might be improper to telephone a young single woman. He sat on the sofa in the living-room and picked up the cordless phone, feeling as if he were Shige's age and had just spotted the girl he secretly loved on the subway platform. *Can't do it*, he muttered to himself and put the phone back down. He opened the drinks cabinet, got out his most expensive bottle of cognac – a *grande champagne* – and poured a glass.

At exactly eight-thirty, before he had a chance to get too drunk, he punched out the number on the handset. Yamasaki Asami answered on the first ring.

'Yes?' she said. Her voice was deeper and thicker than it had been at the audition. Perhaps she'd been dozing.

'Ah, this is Aoyama. One of the producers who interviewed you this afternoon.'

'Oh, hello!' she said, reverting immediately to the crystalline voice that had haunted him all evening. The change was so abrupt that, had he been in a less agitated state of mind, it might have struck him as odd. 'Thank you again for your time today.'

He tried to disguise his nervousness by getting right to the point and keeping things as businesslike as possible.

'I was hoping to talk with you a little more and was wondering if you could find the time. Yoshikawa, the other producer, won't be joining us, so perhaps it might be best to meet during the day. I wouldn't want you to get the wrong idea.'

'I'd be delighted!'

'When would be good for you?'

'Whenever you like. I'm not working daytimes now, so . . .'

'How about the day after tomorrow, then – Thursday, about one p.m.?'

'Perfect!'

He specified a café in one of the high-rise hotels in Akasaka.

After hanging up the phone Aoyama sank back on the sofa, feeling like a balloon in a warm blue sky.

Minutes later, as he was blissfully absorbing his fourth glass of cognac, Yoshikawa called.

'Sorry to disturb you this late in the evening, but something happened that's kind of weighing on my mind.'

'No problem,' Aoyama said. His own voice sounded embarrassingly giddy, as if he'd been inhaling helium.

'Look, it's not that I was suspicious or anything, but after you left I telephoned Victor. Maybe it's no big deal – just some sort of mistake, probably – but there's no producer named Shibata in the domestic music division.'

Aoyama's brandy-soaked brain couldn't make any sense of this at first. *Victor? Shibata?*

'Or rather,' said Yoshikawa, 'not any more, there isn't. A producer named Shibata Hiroshi used to work there, but he died a year and a half ago.'

5

AOYAMA ARRIVED AT THE hotel a full forty minutes early. The café was on the first floor, off the lobby. He'd phoned the day before to reserve a table for one o'clock, as well as a window-side table in a restaurant on the top floor at one-thirty. He had agonised a bit, wondering if a restaurant on the top floor of a high-rise hotel wasn't a bit tacky, if it wouldn't be in better taste to take her for sushi or sukiyaki in the Japanese restaurant in the basement, or to go out to a chic bistro in the town, for example, or a trattoria, or a French restaurant. All day yesterday and all this morning in the office he'd got exactly zero work done. He'd seemed so dazed and distracted, in fact, that several members of his staff had showed concern, asking if he was feeling all right, or if he hadn't better see a doctor.

The café was jammed with the lunch crowd, and he had to stand with the mob near the entrance and wait for his table. He surveyed the lobby to make sure Yamasaki Asami hadn't arrived already. Or, more precisely, to make sure she wasn't watching him stand there like an idiot, fidgeting nervously and checking his watch every few seconds.

'Listen,' Yoshikawa had said on the phone the night before last. 'I know you're pretty far gone, but try to keep your feet on the ground. Don't let her set the pace, whatever you do. We don't know anything for certain about this girl, but I can't shake the feeling that something's wrong here. I'm not saying she was intentionally lying, but, come on, there's something strange about naming a guy who died a year and a half ago as your mentor. He died of a heart problem, apparently, but if he really was her mentor, how could she not know that?'

Aoyama couldn't fathom why Yoshikawa would be suspicious of someone simply because her mentor at a record company had died. What would make him pounce on some trivial detail like that? Why was he being so closed-minded?

An impartial observer might have seen that, in fact, Aoyama was the one whose mind was closed. But he himself was already incapable of being impartial, and it hadn't been only because of the cognac. He'd replied to Yoshikawa's concerns rather testily, insisting that she'd simply mistaken the man's name, and that in any case the question of whether or not she had a mentor or manager or whatever simply wasn't of any importance.

'Yeah, well, anyway,' Yoshikawa had said before hanging up. 'Just watch what you're doing, all right?'

Aoyama was shown to a table next to the floor-to-ceiling windows and ordered iced tea. The café was well heated, and the sunlight through the windows was intense. What with that and the anticipation, he was soon perspiring beneath his shirt and jacket, and his throat was chalk-dry. He glanced around at the other tables, most of which were occupied by large and small groups of middle-aged women: old classmates reuniting, friends from some sports circle or culture club, tourists from the provinces. Every last one of these women seemed to be gabbling at the same time, and the clamour was astonishing. A few scattered tables were occupied by sales-rep types, salarymen out making the rounds of their corporate clients. They all had the body language and wore the suits of men for whom the two-thousand-yen lunch special was exactly right.

The iced tea arrived, and Aoyama drained half of it in two swallows, thinking: *Talk business over two-thousand-yen specials day after day, and you end up coming across like a two-thousand-yen special – nothing fancy, but then again nothing tragic either.* This idle train of thought was abruptly derailed when Yamasaki Asami appeared at the entrance to the café. The instant he saw her, his heart grabbed him by the throat and he realised that the entire list of things he wanted to say – a list he'd gone over several times – had been completely erased from his memory banks. *What's wrong with me?* he had to wonder once again. *Forty-two-year-old men don't act like this.* Yamasaki Asami scanned the room, and when she finally spotted him she beamed and hurried towards his table, threading her way through the waiters and waitresses who bustled back and forth, balancing their trays. Her hair was tied back, as it had been at the audition, and she was dressed in an outfit that managed to be neither flashy nor drab – navy-blue dress, vivid orange scarf, suede jacket and matching pumps, black stockings. This, he thought, was one woman who really understood how best to complement her own beauty. And of course it was clear, from her sense of fashion, that she knew very well how extraordinary her own beauty was.

'Sorry! I'm afraid I'm a little late.'

She sat down across the table from him. The sunlight through the lace curtains both illuminated and veiled her profile. She'd been gorgeous under the bleak fluorescent lights in that meeting room, but in this light, thought Aoyama . . .

She was ten times as beautiful.

'Not at all. I got here much too early. My office is near by.'

He found, to his chagrin, that he couldn't look directly at her and didn't know what to do with his eyes. He felt like a high-school kid, and thought how embarrassed he'd be if Shige were to see him like this. When he tried to focus on that lovely and vaguely melancholy face of hers, it felt as if his heart and stomach were getting all tangled up together. At last he resigned himself to the occasional fleeting glance. If he completely avoided meeting her gaze she might wonder about his character, or even take him for some sort of pervert.

After ordering a lemonade, she tilted her head to one side and smiled.

'I'm really glad to see you again,' she said.

Possibly because she'd hurried for fear of being late, her cheeks were somewhat flushed, and he remembered thinking at the audition that her soul seemed to lie just below the surface of her skin. When she smiled, it was as if you were looking directly at a happy soul. Aoyama decided to peer into her eyes for just a moment each time he began to say something, then look away, but he had to remind himself not to let his gaze dance all over the place. He rested his chin on his left hand, trying to remember if he'd ever been this stiff with tension before. It was exhausting, but exhilarating.

'Please just relax,' he said, thinking, *You're the one who needs to relax, buster*. 'It's not as if I have anything in particular I want to grill you about.'

She nodded and said 'all right' in that voice of hers. That warm, limpid, liquid voice that seemed to curl around his nerve endings.

'I thought we'd have lunch and just, well, chat about this and that. There's a restaurant on the top floor here that I thought might do, but they specialise in steak and so on – are you OK with meat dishes?'

'I like every kind of food.'

Aoyama's palms were moist with perspiration. He was surreptitiously wiping them on his trousers when something very strange occurred. A young man in a wheelchair had entered the café, accompanied by an older woman who was probably his mother. They were laughing about something. Still smiling, the youth turned his head slightly, and his eyes widened as they locked on Yamasaki Asami. The smile froze, the blood drained from his face, and he made as if to rise up from his wheelchair. Seeing his distress, the woman leaned over and asked him, presumably, what was wrong, but he merely shook his head. Averting his gaze and hunching his shoulders as if cowering, he wheeled himself on towards the far end of the room. There was no change whatsoever in Yamasaki Asami's expression as she watched this peculiar little scene play out.

'Someone you know?' Aoyama ventured.

She shook her head and shrugged, apparently just as mystified as he was. The kid must have mistaken her for someone else, Aoyama thought, or maybe he was just having some sort of attack.

He still knew nothing about Yamasaki Asami. But he wasn't going to allow an odd little incident like this – or Yoshikawa's paranoid ravings, for that matter – to burst his bubble.

'I never knew beef could be so delicious!'

At the restaurant, Aoyama had ordered a starter of pigeon pâté, Kobe chateaubriand steak and a half-bottle of red Burgundy. Yamasaki Asami sipped quietly at her wine and responded to his questions in a refreshingly open and natural way. She also ate every last morsel of food she was served. Aoyama, who'd loosened up a little with the wine, liked everything about her. The way she talked, the things she talked about, the way she sipped her wine and handled her fork and knife. He didn't think he'd ever met a woman of whom that was true before.

'This is such a treat!' she said. 'And you really just wanted to chat?'

'Sure.'

'Lucky me!'

'I'm just happy if you're enjoying yourself.'

'How could I not be?' she said. 'Do you come here often?'

'I wouldn't say often. Once in a while. Compared to other places I find it . . . I guess the word would be "genuine".'

'Genuine?'

'Most restaurants of this sort are known for the view, or for their interior design, or their location, and the quality of the food is secondary. But this place isn't like that. Here the atmosphere is designed to enhance the food. They pride themselves on serving the finest meat dishes, and they want you to be as comfortable as possible while enjoying them.'

'It is a nice atmosphere,' she said. 'I suppose only people of the best quality come here.'

'Best quality?'

'People with, well, status.'

'Rich people, you mean?'

'Yes, people with money, and power.'

'Hmm. Well, I don't think of myself as being anything special because I eat in this restaurant. And not all wealthy people are what I would call "quality", believe me.'

'I suppose not,' she said. 'But then again, I wouldn't really know. My father was just a salaryman, and we were just an average middle-class family. We'd spend the day together at one of the big department stores on weekends, and sometimes we'd take trips, but when we ate out it was always at a soba shop or a family restaurant. I guess I grew up believing that places like this – the sorts of restaurants I'd see in magazines – were only for the elite.'

'I don't think that's true any more, if it ever was. Japan has, in an unlikely way, become a wealthy country, and in Tokyo almost anyone can enjoy the best cuisine from all over the world, but . . . It may sound funny for me to say after stuffing myself with a meal like this, but the truth is that we Japanese are more suited to places like soba shops. The food here is fantastic, there's no denying that, but I always feel slightly out of place in this kind of environment.'

She looked down at her plate and smiled.

'I hope this won't sound rude,' she said.

'What?'

'I've never met anyone who says the sorts of things you do.'

'No?'

'I've had, well, only a little experience in the entertainment industry, but the people I've met . . . I can't describe what I mean very well, but everyone seems so . . . arrogant?'

'I don't know. Maybe I'm the one who's got it all wrong. Let me just say, though, that I've never met anyone like you either, Yamasaki-san.'

'Really? In what sense?'

'Most young women who aspire to the entertainment industry are fairly blasé about eating in places like this, for example. Once they've spent a few years with the title "aspiring actress", a lot of these women get pretty hardened without even realising it. They acquire a certain, I don't know, *sordidness* about them. They seem to take it for granted that men will line up to lavish gifts upon them and treat them to expensive meals. My work is mainly documentaries and PR films, but even I see plenty of that hardened, grasping type of young women.'

'I see. Human nature is frightening, isn't it?'

'But you're not like that at all,' he said. 'You're very . . . very *real*.'

She smiled shyly and looked down at the table.

'Thank you,' she said.

It was the first time in ages that Aoyama had shared a deeply satisfying meal with a lady. Yamasaki Asami was even freer of affectation than he'd dared to imagine. And what she said to him as they were leaving the restaurant left him feeling ecstatic.

'I'd like to ask a favour of you,' she said. 'It may seem awfully brazen, but . . . I've been struggling on my own for so long, and I don't really have anyone to talk to and ask for advice. No one mature and trustworthy, at least. I have that mentor at Victor, but the truth is I've never even had direct contact with him, only through a friend of mine. I can't help thinking how wonderful it would be if I could talk things over with someone like you from time to time. I know how busy you must be, and of course I mean only when you have time to spare, and naturally a soba shop or a family restaurant, anywhere at all would be fine, or even over the telephone . . .'

As they waited for the elevator, Aoyama handed her his business card, with the telephone number of his office. She smiled and clasped the card to her heart, as if cradling it. Gazing through the big windows of the elevator hall, Aoyama felt as if he could spread his arms and sail out over the streets of Tokyo.

'I was amazed,' he told Yoshikawa over the telephone as soon as he got back to his office. He was aware of a lingering tension raising the pitch of his voice. 'You just don't find young women like that these days.'

Aoyama recounted the salient points of his conversation with Yamasaki Asami. It seemed as if every word had been engraved in his memory.

'She's so modest and sweet and uncomplicated. Which means, I suppose, that she's not really suited to being an actress, but . . . There's just something very real and solid about her.'

'Oh yeah?' Yoshikawa said in a rather cold tone of voice. 'Well, I have to be a wet blanket, but you know where I stand on this. Something doesn't seem right about this woman. You didn't tell her the real purpose of the audition, did you?'

'Of course not,' Aoyama said with some asperity. Yoshikawa didn't understand, but then Yoshikawa hadn't shared a lunch with her. Maybe he was just envious. Aoyama had exceeded both their expectations, after all, by finding what looked to be the ideal woman.

'I found out a little more about this Shibata character at Victor,' Yoshikawa said, and Aoyama groaned inwardly. 'He produced a number of hits in the seventies. Fairly well respected in the industry, but there was always a lot of talk about his womanising. Granted, there's nothing unusual about a record producer taking on singers or actresses as protégées, or privately handling their management for them, or, let's face it, privately handling their bodies once in a while. But it seems that once Shibata lost most of his power in the industry – especially during the last few years of his career – he used the mentor thing exclusively for the purpose of getting laid. Apparently to the point that it caused serious trouble for Victor. Of course, there are creeps like that at any record company, but . . . Did you ask her about this guy at all?'

'Of course I did,' Aoyama said angrily. 'Yoshikawa, listen. She only had contact with Shibata through an acquaintance of hers. She never even met him.'

'Is that so?'

'Look. If Shibata was such a womaniser, he probably had a little black book full of protégées and potential protégées, right?'

'Good chance.'

'So he probably just never got around to calling her. Which would explain why she didn't know he was

83

dead, and why no one else at the company would know about her.'

Yoshikawa's 'hmph' was somewhere between a grunt and a scornful laugh. Aoyama was seething. He'd been particularly offended by that 'privately handling their bodies' crack. Just to picture some arrogant, bloated, middle-aged record producer putting his arm around Yamasaki Asami's shoulder, whispering 'Unnerstand?' or 'That's a good girl', had twisted his stomach into a knot.

'There's something else, too,' Yoshikawa said in the same cool-to-cold tone. 'Her family in Suginami? They aren't there any more. Moved away two years ago. I had a girl in my office try to contact them – same as we would for any finalist – and they're gone.'

'People move house all the time,' Aoyama spat. Why was Yoshikawa investigating every little thing?

'True. But the landlord didn't even know where they'd moved to. Normally you leave a forwarding address, right? For mail and whatnot?'

'They must've had their reasons.'

'No doubt.' Spoken with a tinge of sarcasm.

'Yoshikawa, I appreciate your concern, but I've already made up my mind. To tell you the truth, I'm not the least bit interested in any of the other women, and I couldn't care less about the film.'

'Now, wait just a minute—'

'Don't worry, I'm not going to leave you hanging. Just tell me what you need me to do. You can have my rights to the story idea for free, and I'll fix it up with the Germans too. But I've already found what I was looking for, and then some. I wish you'd just accept that and be happy for me. In any case, I have no motivation for continuing with the movie project now, and I'd like to disengage myself from the production side. You can understand that, can't you?'

Yoshikawa was silent for a moment. Then he sighed and spoke in an even colder tone.

'I don't give a shit about the film either. Calm down a minute and listen to me, all right? I'll take care of the movie, that's not the problem. What I'm worried about is you. Maybe you're right, and there's nothing to the Shibata question or the disappearing family. I mean, you're probably right about that, but something feels screwy. Think about it. As of right now, we have no one who knows anything at all about this woman. I'm probably overreacting, and maybe it seems like I'm being a pain in the ass. And I'm not going to pretend that I'm not a little envious that a guy my age can hook up with such a knock-out. But I'm only trying to be as honest and objective as possible. Can't you see that?'

'I guess so.' As Aoyama said this he flashed on the strange incident of the young man in the wheelchair, but only for a moment. His psychological defences had encircled the euphoric glow left over from lunch with

Yamasaki Asami. He'd never imagined he could derive so much pleasure simply from being with someone, and he wasn't interested in entertaining any doubts. The memory of the kid in the wheelchair was pushed aside as soon as it arose, and nothing Yoshikawa said was making any real impression on him.

'Anyway, I'm not saying there's anything in particular that I'm worried about, it's just a feeling. You're in the clouds over this woman, and that's not a bad thing. Seriously, I'm not being sarcastic. It's important to enjoy life. But the way I look at it, life is never all that easy. A woman of that calibre remaining unspoken for . . . Well, it's all just a little too perfect, if you ask me. And it bothers me that we don't really know anything about her. It's exactly the sort of situation that could get messy. So listen, do me one favour. You gave her your number, right? My hunch is that if you don't contact her for a week or so, she'll contact you. If she does, be on your guard; if not, go ahead and call her. But give it at least a week. All right?'

A week passed, and there was no communication from Yamasaki Asami. Partly because of his own sense that a man shouldn't appear over-anxious, Aoyama did as Yoshikawa had asked and then went one further by waiting an extra week. But in those two weeks he thought of nothing but her, to the extent that not only his staff but Shige and even Rie-san began to ask if he

86

was sure he was feeling all right. He lost weight, too –
three full kilos.

On the fifteenth day, after conferring with Yoshikawa, he called her.

'Thank goodness,' she said, in that spine-melting
voice. 'I was beginning to think I wouldn't hear from
you!'

6

'I HOPE THIS WON'T sound too pathetic, but I've been waiting every day for you to call.'

Each syllable uttered in that voice was a gemlike particle that rolled through the receiver, into the ear canal and straight to the brain. His spine went numb and a sweet sensation seeped through his body, as if he were absorbing some exquisite wine or cognac. Why had he been such a fool as to leave her hanging for two whole weeks? He pictured her sitting up each night alone, hugging her knees, waiting for the phone to ring. The picture was like a knife in his heart.

'It's been crazy here,' he said hoarsely. He felt as if he were producing the words not so much by vibrating his vocal cords as by wringing them out of his throat. 'I just couldn't find the time.'

'I understand. I was thinking that you must be awfully busy.'

Aoyama was at a loss as to what to say. He wished he could simply fold her in his arms.

'So, how have you been?' he said, and immediately thought, *Idiot!*

'Fine. Hanging in there.'

'I'm sorry I didn't call sooner.'

'That's all right,' she said. 'It's good to hear your voice.'

They were both silent for a moment. Aoyama could hear her breathing softly.

'But I hope you'll always feel free to call,' she said. 'Whenever you're not too busy, I mean.'

'I gave you my card, didn't I? You could have called me.'

'Is it really all right?'

'Of course it is. But listen, why don't we have dinner sometime soon?'

'Really?'

'What nights are you free?'

'I only work on Tuesdays, Thursdays and Fridays.'

'How about Wednesday, then?'

'I can't wait!'

After arranging the time and place, Aoyama hung up and took several deep breaths. He noticed that his cheeks had relaxed into a smile. He heard her voice, her words, echoing over and over again in his head: *I can't wait, I can't wait, I can't wait . . .*

'What's up with you lately, Pops?'

It was the night before his second date with Yamasaki Asami. He and Shige were eating dinner and watching an NBA game on TV. Rie-san had prepared shrimp dumplings, a beef and potato stew, and vegetable soup. The game was a premier match-up: the Chicago Bulls versus the Orlando Magic.

'What's up with me? What are you talking about?'

Aoyama had a glass of beer in his left hand and a dumpling scissored between chopsticks in his right. But he'd held them like that for the past minute or so without wetting his lips or taking a bite, and the dumpling was out of steam and looked in danger of falling to the carpet. His eyes were on the TV screen, but they hadn't been following the movements of Michael Jordan or Penny Hardaway. He'd been day-dreaming about Yamasaki Asami.

'Come on. You're not even paying attention to the game. It's like you're in a trance.'

Whoops, thought Aoyama, plopping the dumpling in his mouth. But all he said was, 'Oh?'

'Yeah. You're acting really weird. Holding that dumpling up in mid-air, with your eyes all out of focus. Why don't you go in for a check-up?'

'There's nothing wrong with me. Don't worry.'

'People don't always know when they're sick. You ever see *Awakenings* with Robert De Niro, or Dustin Hoffman in *Rainman*? You remind me of one of those guys. Maybe you're getting Alzheimer's, or that disease where your brain turns to sponge.'

'Sponge?'

'There's this thing called a prion that eats away at your brain until it ends up riddled with little holes, like a sponge, or a pumice stone.'

'Quite the expert, aren't you?'

'I told you I like biology, but never mind about me. Get yourself to a hospital.'

'This disease is something they can cure at a hospital?'

'Not even.'

'So what's the use of going?'

'Yeah, but think about me. I just entered high school. Can't have you turning into Rainman on me. I'm way too busy to be playing nurse for my old man.'

Shige didn't so much as crack a smile as he said this. Aoyama laughed and took a sip of his beer. He wondered if he should tell him about Yamasaki Asami. He'd have to sooner or later. On TV, the Bulls were expanding their lead. Dennis Rodman, his hair dyed green, grabbed a rebound and fired it out to Jordan, who drove hard to the basket, drawing three defenders, then dished to Scottie Pippen for the slam dunk. It was likely that before very long Yamasaki Asami would be sharing these evening meals with them. Shige had a right to know that, Aoyama reminded himself, and maybe now was a good opportunity to discuss things. Besides, it would save him from having to lie about his date tomorrow.

'There's something I need to tell you,' he said. Shige read the tone in his voice and laid down his chopsticks.

Aoyama said he'd met a woman through work, and outlined the situation without specifically mentioning the audition.

'How old is she?' Shige said when he was done.

'Twenty-four, I think.'

'Pretty young.'

'Yeah.'

'Closer to my age than yours. I hope you know what you're doing, Pops. Quite a babe, is she?'

'You hope I know what I'm doing?'

'You're sure she's not taking you for a ride?'

'Look, I just met this woman. Tomorrow we're having dinner together, but that'll only be the third time I've seen her.'

'You have to watch your step with women these days, Pops. She could be involved with yakuza or something. Even some of the girls in my class – you should hear the stuff they talk about. Fifteen years old, and there's nothing they don't know. We're not in the age of Peace and Love any more.'

'You just can't imagine that a young woman would find me attractive, can you?'

'It's not that. All I'm saying is that you're a little brain-dead right now. I look at the girls in my class, and there's something, like, mercenary about them. I mean, I don't even understand some of the things they're into. There's this girl in the class ahead of me who just got kicked out of school for working at an S&M club. Can you believe that? I've started to think I'll find myself a nice girl from Kazakhstan or somewhere. Language might be a problem, but—'

'Kazakhstan?'

'The women there are supposed to be beautiful, with really excellent personalities.'

'Sounds like you've given this quite a bit of thought.'

'We talked about this before, remember? I said there were hardly any good-looking girls in my class, and you said beautiful women were as rare as stag beetles?'

'Right.'

'But a beautiful woman with a good personality, good character, is hundreds of times harder to find than a stag beetle. More like the Japanese wildcat, or the giant salamander, or the crested ibis.'

On TV, the Magic had begun a rally. Hardaway made three consecutive three-point shots.

'I'll introduce you to her eventually.'

'Yeah, I'll check her out for you,' Shige said, without losing the look of serious concern on his face. 'I think I'll be able to read her better than you can, Pops. Not just because she's nearer my age, but, like I said, you're basically brain-dead right now.'

They'd arranged to meet at the same hotel café at six p.m. He got there twenty minutes early, and at five to six he saw her arrive. Her hair was pulled back in a tight knot, and she was wearing a soft turtleneck sweater and loose-fitting pants, with a leather jacket draped over her left arm – impeccable fashion for the time and place. Aoyama could feel the excitement building inside him again, but he kept reminding himself of the decision he'd made after talking to Shige. He wanted to ask Yamasaki Asami about her private life, and he wanted to do so before dinner and the attendant accumulation of alcohol. He couldn't actually imagine that she was involved with yakuza or anything of that sort – and even in the unlikely event that she was, he had plenty of acquaintances, beginning with Yoshikawa, who knew how to handle such situations. But talking with Shige had brought home to Aoyama the fact that he himself wasn't exactly a kid any more, even if he felt like one. He knew – and anyone with eyes could see – that he was in love with this woman. She, for her part, had been thrilled when he called, and now she was showing up for their date dressed to perfection and beaming an apparently irrepressible smile. It was unthinkable that she was faking all this, but it *was* possible that her intentions were different from his – that she was thinking of him not as a man so much as simply a reliable, mature person to confide in. He'd managed just enough objectivity the night before to consider this possibility.

'I'm having a beer. What would you like?'

She took a seat across from him and bowed her head slightly, still smiling in a way that manifestly revealed her to be beside herself with joy but somewhat embarrassed about feeling that way. If this was an act, Aoyama thought, the girl was a genius.

'I'll have a beer too,' she said quietly, then shook her head and laughed.

'What's so funny?' Aoyama asked, smiling in spite of himself.

'I'm sorry. I really didn't think we'd meet again like this, so . . . I'm just happy.'

The waiter brought another beer and poured it for her.

'I made a reservation at an Italian place I'm fond of,' Aoyama said. 'But I couldn't get a table until seven-thirty. Can you wait that long to eat?'

'Of course.'

They touched glasses, and Aoyama decided to get straight to it.

'Yamasaki-san,' he said, 'I haven't asked you anything about your family. Are they all well?'

The smile vanished as if turned off with a switch. Her face went pale, and she pressed her lips tightly together. Yoshikawa's words reverberated in Aoyama's brain: *As of right now, we have no one who knows anything at all about this woman.* Was he about to catch her in a lie, before he'd ever kissed her or even held her hand? Maybe she *was* hiding something. Maybe it was all some sort of scam after all.

'I don't want to keep anything from you,' she said, 'so I'm going to tell you the truth – all of it.'

Aoyama braced himself. His heart was pounding so hard he wondered if the lapels of his jacket weren't bouncing up and down. His complete attention was riveted on her, and everything else around them ceased to exist.

'My parents divorced when I was small – I don't even have any memory of it – and I was sent to live with my mother's younger brother. All I remember about that time is being terribly mistreated, mostly by my uncle's wife. She was just that sort of person, I guess. She . . . This isn't a pretty story, and it might not be pleasant to hear, but it's the truth, so . . .'

Aoyama nodded and shifted in his chair.

'My uncle's wife once bathed me in cold water – this was in the wintertime – and I ended up coming down with pneumonia. Another time she slammed my head into a window, and I got a big gash on my forehead and bled so much I thought I was dying. And she once pushed me down the stairs. It could have killed me, I think, but all I got was a dislocated shoulder. As a little girl, I always had some sort of wound or bruise or broken bone, but when I was in elementary school a doctor became concerned enough to intervene, and I was sent back to my mother. Mother had remarried, and her new husband . . . well, he was my stepfather, of course, but even now I can't think of him as any kind of father to me. I hate to say that, but it's true.'

She fell silent for a moment, as if waiting to build up the strength to continue. Aoyama's heart was hammering even harder now. He hadn't expected to hear anything like this, and it froze his blood just to imagine her suffering the sort of abuse she was describing.

'My mother's new husband didn't beat me every day, the way my uncle's wife did, but he used to say things like, "You disgust me. Just looking at you leaves a bad taste in my mouth." Things like that. "I hate you. I'd just as soon kill you as look at you. You smell bad, too," he'd say. He wouldn't have me in the same room as them, even during dinner. As soon as I got home from school, he'd tell me to go to the other room. It felt bad, of course, but I didn't know any better, and I guess I just thought that this was the way life was. My mother never tried to protect me and never even said she was sorry about what was happening. It . . . it mystifies me to think about that now. But the truth is, the fact that she never apologised to me was a blessing, in a way, because it helped me, or forced me, to be strong. If she'd ever said, "I'm sorry, honey," I think it would have been even harder for me, though I can't say exactly why. I still see my mother sometimes, we'll meet for tea, but once, quite a while ago now, we were drinking together – my mother's a big drinker – and she said something I've never forgotten. Her own mother, my grandmother, was an alcoholic too, and apparently she was married and divorced several times. My mother said she'd always wanted to live a life completely different from the one her own mother had led. But she said she hadn't been able to after all.'

When he noticed the tears welling up in her eyes, Aoyama's chest constricted. Not just figuratively, either – it was as if someone were tightening an invisible corset around his ribs. She bit her lips to hold back the tears, and after a moment she continued her story.

'She said that even though she was able to picture a different life, she wasn't strong enough to make it a reality. She told me that real strength is the capacity for kindness to others, and that I should do whatever I could to find that kind of strength. She said she couldn't tell me how to go about doing that, because she never found it herself, but that people who were strong enough to be kind to others could always get by in this world. My mother's new husband was handicapped – he didn't have the use of his legs – and for some reason I was always a fast runner. Mother said maybe that was why he hated me so much, but . . .'

Aoyama quietly took a few deep breaths. Her confession explained a lot, and he was aware of a certain

sense of relief, among all the other emotions. Undoubt-
edly her mother and the 'new husband' had been living
in the apartment in Suginami. Though they were
probably her parents legally, she wasn't in regular
contact with them, which would account for her
not knowing they'd moved. Why should she care?

'The last time you were kind enough to meet with
me,' she said, 'I'm afraid I told you a lie. I said that we
sometimes went to soba shops or family restaurants
together, but the truth is we never went anywhere as a
family. It wasn't easy for my mother's new husband to
get around, for one thing, and I wasn't allowed to eat
meals with them even at home. Well, I did share a meal
with my mother from time to time, but . . . Here
you've been so kind to me, and what do I do but
lie to you the first time we get a chance to talk? I know
there's no excuse for that. If you want me to leave
now, please just say so.'

Aoyama looked into her eyes. She was clearly holding back the tears through sheer force of will. He
searched for the right words to say, and finally decided
just to express his feelings honestly, without embellish-
ment.

'I don't know what I'd do if you left,' he said. 'You
have no idea how much I've been looking forward to
seeing you. And what you've just told me doesn't
change anything.'

She nodded deeply, and quietly began to weep.

In the taxi later, en route to the restaurant in Nishi-Azabu, Aoyama said there was just one thing he didn't understand.

'Ask me anything,' she said. 'I'd die rather than hide anything from you ever again.'

It was as if her confession had relieved her of a burden. She sat relaxed, casually leaning towards him in the seat. Aoyama, too, strangely enough, was much more relaxed now. He thought it must be because they'd shared something so intimate, and so powerful.

'I'm no expert,' he said, 'but obviously you suffered severe abuse as a child, both physical and emotional. And to my knowledge, people with that sort of background generally have a difficult time relating to others. They tend to be riddled with complexes and basically unpleasant to be around. I once read that when victims of child abuse grow up they unconsciously do things to make other people dislike them, because they actually feel more at ease being disliked, which makes a certain twisted sort of sense, I suppose. But you're not like that at all. You don't seem like someone who's been – how to put this? – scarred by it all.'

She nodded several times, as if to herself, then leaned against him and said in a barely audible voice, 'Thank you.' Her face was close to his, and as he looked at her long, drooping eyelashes, a tremor ran down his spine.

The restaurant was on a relatively quiet little street just up the hill from the Nishi-Azabu intersection. It was famous for its Tuscan cuisine, but it wasn't listed in guidebooks, and the management actually discouraged media coverage. The interior was immaculate, the service was excellent, and none of the diners looked as if they'd stumbled into the wrong place. Anyone coming here for the first time would experience, if not awe, at least a pleasant sort of tension on seeing the exquisite engraved designs on the glass partitions around each table and the magnificent tapestry, of which the manager was especially proud – it depicted seventeenth-century Florence and covered one entire wall. It was not a large place, and you couldn't get reservations without a formal introduction from a trusted customer. Yamasaki Asami's eyes sparkled as they sat down. When the waiter asked if they'd like an aperitif, she ordered a Campari and orange in an appealingly girlish voice and looked at Aoyama as if to ask if she wasn't making a faux pas. He winked at her reassuringly and ordered the carpaccio, a speciality of the house, and another starter consisting of three types of pasta. He chose Florentine T-bone steak for the main course, and a bottle of 1989 Barbaresco.

The aperitifs arrived, and Yamasaki Asami took a sip of her Campari.

'I think it's because of ballet,' she said. For a moment Aoyama had no idea what she was talking about.

'You mentioned that I don't seem scarred by the abuse. I was really glad to hear you say that, and I think it's true, but it made me wonder: why is it that I don't still carry the scars? I thought about it when we were in the taxi but couldn't really come up with a good answer. And then, when we came in here, it's such a fantastic place . . .'

She paused and smiled. It was a perfect smile, Aoyama thought. Who wouldn't be enchanted by this smile?

'I guess my attention span isn't all it might be,' she said, 'but maybe that's one reason I don't get too depressed about things. When we sat down here, and I saw this tablecloth, and these candlesticks and napkins, and especially the beautiful designs on this glass – these grapes and the little birds and these musical instruments, the curving lines . . . Do you think they're all handmade? The designs are different at each table.'

'I wonder. Maybe they *are* engraved by hand.'

'I'm sure of it. They're so warm and intimate . . . Anyway, as I was looking at all these things, forgetting all about my question, the answer popped into my mind: ballet.'

'So you're saying that ballet helped you heal the scars?'

'Yes. I was in the fourth grade, and we were living in that small apartment in Suginami. Just down the street was a little ballet school, run by an elderly woman and her daughter. The lessons were cheap, and my mother suggested I give it a try. Apparently I have the right build for ballet – at least, that's what I was told – and after a year the teacher, the elderly one, told me I should switch to a bigger school. She wrote a letter of introduction for me, and I ended up getting a scholarship to a place in Minami-Aoyama, one of the biggest ballet studios in Japan.'

She looked down at the tablecloth, and Aoyama waited for her to continue.

'I don't know how to express this very well,' she said, 'but when you work up a sweat dancing, it's as if all the bad things, all the bad thoughts, pour out of you. You can almost see them evaporating. You know the big mirrors they have in dance studios? When I'd watch myself in the mirror after mastering a new *pas*, a new step, I'd feel, well, purified. To see that I was able to some extent to become one with something beautiful, with this graceful image I had in my head, was . . . Well, I can't explain it. But it helped me forget my troubles, and I think that's how I managed to overcome it all.'

The sommelier uncorked the Barbaresco, freeing its distinctive bouquet, and poured some into Aoyama's glass. As he took a sip and rolled it over his tongue, he had to make an effort to stifle the tears. He nodded, and the sommelier retreated. A waiter placed the carpaccio on the table before them, and when they were left alone again, all Aoyama could manage to say was, 'I see.'

A moment later he added: 'You're amazing.'

They clinked their glasses in a toast.

'You really do understand, don't you?' she said. 'That makes me so happy. I put everything I had into ballet, for so long, but there was no one I could really talk to. And after I hurt my hip . . . It's not that I don't have friends, or many opportunities to meet people, but there was no one really to comfort me. In fact, you're the first person I've ever talked to like this, about my mother's new husband and everything. I've never told anyone about these things, ever . . .'

7

AOYAMA ESCORTED HER HOME in a taxi. They'd taken
their time during the meal, following the wine with
grappa and lingering over dessert, and now it was past
eleven. He was sure she'd gladly have gone along if
he'd suggested they have another drink somewhere,
but he felt that dinner was enough for tonight. The
exhilarating sort of tension he'd experienced for the
past five hours was taking its toll, and besides, he
didn't want to press his luck. How much happiness,
after all, would the gods allow one man?

Mushy with wine and grappa, he wanted to hold her
hand in the taxi, but decided after some mental wres-
tling to resist that impulse too. And thought: a 42-
year-old man who frets over whether or not to hold
hands – how ridiculous is that?

'Let's have dinner again soon,' he said when the taxi
stopped to let her out near Nakameguro station.

'When?' she said immediately, then looked embarrassed at having let her eagerness show. Like a child

caught in some harmless mischief. The subtle play of facial expressions – the momentary blush of embarrassment, followed immediately by a droop of the head and a smile that betrayed the joy bubbling up inside her – was more eloquent than any words, and Aoyama found it intoxicating.

'I'll call you,' he said, and she quietly replied:

'I'll be waiting.'

'Sorry to bother you so late.'

He was using his mobile to telephone Yoshikawa on the way home. He could scarcely believe how well the date had gone. The back seat of the taxi might as well have been a cloud, and he felt as if the blood in his veins had turned to honey. Catching a whiff of her cologne on the headrest beside him, he remembered agonising over whether or not to hold her hand. But his euphoria painted the memory in a romantic light and reassured him that love could make a man feel that way, even a man his age. He'd taken the phone from his briefcase thinking he'd like to share these feelings with all the forty-something men of the world, but of course Yoshikawa was the only one he could actually call.

'Were you sleeping?'

'What's up? It's nearly midnight.'

Yoshikawa sounded tired. Or possibly drunk. Aoyama had been to his house a few times, and imagined him sitting in his narrow den, drinking Cordon Bleu after the wife and kid had gone to bed. He would have taken the bottle and a glass from the shelves that also held his golf trophies, sliced himself a little cheese in the kitchen, and sat down to pass some quiet time with a magazine or a video. Poor bastard, thought Aoyama – getting drunk all alone before bed. I have to let him know that being middle-aged doesn't mean all your opportunities are behind you, that you can't just give up.

'I had a date tonight.' Aoyama tried to keep the elation out of his voice.

'Oh yeah? And?'

'Learned all about her sublime past.'

'Such as?'

'I can't give you the details – it's very personal stuff – but I can tell you she had an incredibly difficult childhood and managed to rise above it, all on her own. Of course, that may not mean much to a cynic like you . . .'

He paused, but Yoshikawa didn't say anything.

'Hello? You there?'

'I'm here.'

The irritation in Yoshikawa's voice dampened the euphoria somewhat. Why couldn't the bastard rejoice a little over his friend's good fortune? Aoyama remembered reading an article by a famous lady columnist about how our ability to feel and express emotions – to distort our faces with joy, or wail and weep with sorrow, or collapse in agony, or wallow

107

in sentimentality – wasn't an inviolable human trait but something we can lose simply by leading dull and dreary lives. 'A rich emotional life,' she'd written, 'is a privilege reserved only for the daring few.' Maybe Yoshikawa just wasn't one of the few.

'Anyway, I was really impressed.'

'That's great,' Yoshikawa said.

On the other hand, maybe it wasn't just irritation. He sounded almost despondent.

'Anything wrong?'

Yoshikawa didn't answer. Aoyama wondered if he should cut the conversation short.

'Well, I'll call again some other—'

'No, no, it's all right. I just . . . I didn't want to bring you down when you're in such a good mood, is all. My mother – you met her, right?'

'Of course. Did something happen?' She must've died, thought Aoyama. Good grief. He calls to send glad tidings from the mountaintop and his friend is sinking in the abyss. 'Don't tell me . . .'

'No, it's not that. Just the old story – getting a little senile, and now she falls down the stairs. I'm telling you, there are times you think we'd all be better off if she'd just . . . Sorry. Pretty grim stuff, I know.'

'I'm the one who should apologise. Calling you about something like this, when—'

'Hey, I'm happy for the distraction. It has been pretty depressing, though. I mean, you always hear that once the dementia starts they can become like a completely different person, but when it's your mother . . . Of course, the one who's really suffering is my wife. I should've moved my mother into a home of some sort right from the beginning. But I kept procrastinating, and the next thing I know seven years have gone by. Terrible thing to do to her – my wife, I mean. She worries more about the old lady than I do, even. Sometimes she bursts into tears and says it's her fault. Of course, she and my mother have a sort of bond that I don't even completely understand.'

'She's all right, though, isn't she? Your mother.'

'Yeah. It's just her leg. My wife's with her at the hospital right now. Her legs were shot anyway, but she broke an ankle. It's not like when you're young and it breaks cleanly, you know. Apparently the doctor's colourful explanation was that it looked like someone had taken a hammer to a brick of charcoal. Just powdered, in other words, and no chance that it'll ever be whole again. I was sitting here thinking, well, it looks like there's no choice now but to put her in a home, but then I had a drink or two, and . . . What a loser, eh?'

'Don't say shit like that.'

'There are great places nowadays, you know, with round-the-clock care.'

'Yeah. I've seen pamphlets.'

'They're not cheap, but . . . Well. Sorry to lay all this on you.'

'I don't mind.'

'I envy you, Aoyama. Same age as me, and look at the difference. Dating a 24-year-old.'

Aoyama didn't reply. His friend, the very one who'd created the opportunity for him to meet Yamasaki Asami, was suffering. He wanted to say something helpful but was still under the influence of his euphoria, and it wasn't easy to empathise with someone else's depression.

'Oh, by the way,' Yoshikawa said, then fell silent a moment and sighed. 'Nah, never mind. It doesn't matter.'

'What.'

'Nothing. Forget it.'

'Just say it.'

'It's just a stupid rumour I heard. From a hostess in a bar, no less. Not exactly a reliable source.'

'Go on.'

'It's about that guy at the record company, Shibata. Speaking of legs.'

Legs? Hearing the name Shibata brought Aoyama crashing to earth. The womanising record producer who'd had an indirect connection to Yamasaki Asami. Or had there in fact been more to their relationship? Just to think of that possibility filled him with hatred for the man. Shibata had probably wined and dined beautiful young women on a nightly basis. Someone of his ilk wouldn't have agonised, as Aoyama had, about holding

Yamasaki Asami's hand. He'd have been all over her at the first opportunity. Aoyama felt as if he could murder a slimeball like that. Thankfully Shibata was already dead.

'Supposedly he was from a pretty well-connected family, and things were hushed up to prevent a scandal, but . . . Well, according to the rumour his heart attack was caused by someone trying to cut off his feet, from the ankles down. In other words he was murdered, supposedly, but again, I got this from a bar hostess. Sounds like something out of *Friday the 13th*. Probably not even worth checking out.'

Aoyama was relieved. At least the rumour had nothing to do with Yamasaki Asami. And if it was true, he thought, the bastard only got what was coming to him. Aoyama's euphoria and jealousy joined forces with the alcohol to banish the whole matter from his mind, and he didn't give it another thought. Nor, unfortunately, did he make any connection to the youth in the wheelchair, in the hotel café.

'Oh, it's you, Pops. The way Gangsta was carrying on, I thought it must be a burglar or something.'

Aoyama had opened the front door to find Shige standing there in his pyjamas, with a combat knife in his hand.

'Where the hell did you get that thing?'

It was a big knife, with a blade about thirty centimetres long.

'You don't remember? You bought it yourself, Pops, in Singapore or Hong Kong or somewhere.'

'I'll be damned,' Aoyama said, walking through the living-room to the kitchen. 'You're right.'

About ten years ago he'd travelled in South-East Asia. It was at an open-air market in Manila, if he remembered correctly, that he'd purchased the knife on a whim. Ryoko had confiscated the weapon, scolding him for bringing such a dangerous thing into the house, and he hadn't seen it or thought about it since.

'Where was it?' He selected a cold Evian from the refrigerator, came back to the living-room, plopped down on the sofa and took a swig.

'I just found it recently,' Shige said, sliding the knife back into its hard plastic sheath.

'Where?'

'In the drinks cabinet.'

'I never noticed it.'

'In the bottom part, where the expensive wine is? It was behind all the bottles. That's Mum for you.'

The bottom compartment had double doors and a built-in lock, and it was there that Aoyama stored the Château d'Yquem and Romanée-Conti and other famous wines he brought back each time he went to Europe on business. He had a collection of fourteen or fifteen bona fide monsters.

'What do you mean?'

'She never throws anything away,' Shige said, keeping it in the present tense. 'She might get mad and say she's going to toss something, but she can't do it.'

'That's true.' Aoyama nodded, lowering his eyes and smiling. They were both silent for a moment. He was picturing Ryoko's face and imagined Shige was doing the same.

'It's not even rusty or anything,' Shige said. 'Perfect place to store it, really. No humidity.'

'When did you find it?'

'Couple of months ago. Remember when that friend of mine stayed over? The tall, skinny guy?'

Shige was popular in school and his friends often spent the night at their house. Aoyama tended to make himself scarce when that happened, but Rie-san always enjoyed taking charge and preparing lots of food for the boys – rice curry and sushi rolls and spaghetti and so on.

'He's really into wine.'

'Wine? A first-year high-school student?'

'Yeah. He wants to be a . . . what do you call those guys?'

'A sommelier?'

'Right. Said he wanted to see your collection.'

'At fifteen he's already decided what he wants to be?'

'Lots of guys have.'

113

'Is that wise? To limit your options at such a young age?'

'Welcome to the new world, Pops. It's not like the golden days of your youth. The world's gone to hell, right? Corruption and everything.'

'True.'

'Anybody with a brain knows that attaining success in this country doesn't amount to squat. I think the wine thing is a good idea, something practical you can really focus on and get engrossed in. Lots of guys my age have already decided what they want to do – software engineer, that's a big one, graphic design . . . Well, mostly computer-related stuff, I guess. But if you're going to specialise in something it's best to get started early, right?'

'And you?'

'I've decided to hold off a while longer. I like biology, and chemistry, but I haven't had any biochemistry or molecular biology or anything like that yet, so. . .'

Shige put the knife back in the cabinet and returned the key to its hiding-place beneath a bottle of armagnac.

'Don't even think about ever using that in a fight,' Aoyama said. Shige rolled his eyes. 'Even against intruders or whatever. Sometimes having a weapon can put you in greater danger.'

'I know that. But when Gangsta starts barking and

114

I'm all alone in the house . . . You know, there've been a lot of burglaries around here lately.'

Aoyama looked at the clock. It was nearly one a.m., and he felt a little guilty about having left Shige alone while he was out enjoying himself. He finished off his Evian and said, 'I'll try not to stay out so late from now on.'

'How did it go, by the way?' Shige said, heading back upstairs.

'What?'

'Your date.'

'Oh. It was good. She had a pretty unfortunate childhood, and I heard a lot of the details tonight. Grew up in an abusive family, with no one to turn to. But the thing is, she managed to overcome it all through ballet. Most beautiful women are pampered all their lives, but she had to learn to be strong and rely on herself.'

Shige stopped halfway up the stairs and looked down at him.

'What?' Aoyama said.

Shige shrugged.

'I don't know anything about ballet,' he said, 'but from what I hear it's not that easy to overcome being abused as a child.'

Aoyama marvelled for the thousandth time at how mature his son was becoming. He smiled and said goodnight, telling himself that Shige would understand when he met her.

'Good night, Pops,' Shige said from the top of the stairs. His voice was as gentle and assured as that of a grown man.

Autumn was turning to winter. The FM programme *Tomorrow's Heroine* was dying a quiet death. Yoshikawa said that, when it finally expired, all they had to do was announce that because of script considerations all further auditions were being postponed. There wouldn't be any problem whatsoever, he said – dozens of film projects got cancelled each year.

'Besides, we're not film producers, so it's not as if our reputations are on the line. Give it two weeks and nobody'll even remember the whole thing anyway.' Yoshikawa was in better spirits these days. He'd moved his mother into a nursing home on the outskirts of Tokyo. 'But you've got a bit of a challenge ahead,' he said. 'Obviously you'll have to tell the lovely Yamasaki-san that the film is officially kaput. You haven't slept with her yet, have you? I don't care how sweet she is, to sleep with her before confessing the truth would be asking for trouble.'

Aoyama still hadn't even held hands with her.

They'd had four or five more dates over the past couple of months. And though they'd yet to go beyond dinner and drinks, he could tell she enjoyed being with him. Her voice was always vibrant and animated when he called, and she showed up for their dates in flawless fashion and make-up. He, for his part, grew more besotted with her each time they met. He took her to the best restaurants he knew of and introduced her to a series of serious wines. They'd spend hours over each meal, engaging in a regular feast of reason and flow of soul. She never tired of talking about ballet, and he often waxed poetic on his reminiscences of Germany, and yet the conversation always seemed sparkling and new.

But as the final episode of *Tomorrow's Heroine* neared, Aoyama began to feel the pressure. When should he break the news that the film project had fallen through? That wasn't the only thing he needed to discuss with her, either. She still didn't know much about his own personal life. Somehow he had yet to find the right opportunity to reveal that he'd lost his wife seven years before and lived with his fifteen-year-old son. And she seemed to take great care not to ask about such matters.

It was late October, a week before the final instalment of the radio show, on an evening when the first blasts of wintry wind were strafing Tokyo, that Aoyama decided it was time.

He'd asked her to meet him at the bar in one of the high-rise hotels in West Shinjuku. He wanted to tell her about the film project before they went to dinner, and in order to collect his thoughts he arrived almost twenty minutes early. The bar here specialised in champagne – even serving it by the glass – and had become a bit of a hot spot after being written up in a few trendy magazines. This early in the evening, however, it was still half-empty. The waiter greeted Aoyama by name and offered a table, but he chose to sit at the bar. He preferred not to be facing Yamasaki Asami when he told her the news.

She glided in wearing a black minidress and boots, and, as always, the head of every man in the place turned as she passed.

'I haven't been to Shinjuku in ages.' She smiled and eased on to the stool beside him.

'I know this unique little restaurant not far from here,' he said, 'in East Nakano. It's run by a former geisha, and she serves authentic Edo *kuruwa* cuisine. I thought it might be a nice change.'

'Everywhere we go, the food's so irresistible.' She patted her very narrow waist. 'I'm afraid I've been gaining weight.'

Aoyama grinned and ordered Dom Pérignon rosé for both of them. After a casual toast and a swallow, he braced himself and dived in.

'I'm afraid I have some unfortunate news tonight,' he said. She was lowering her glass to the counter but froze halfway there, her features visibly stiffening.

'What is it?' she whispered.

The plan was to explain the situation roughly along the semi-truthful lines Yoshikawa had suggested. Aoyama looked down at his glass of champagne and concentrated on suppressing an incipient tremor in his voice.

'It's about the film you auditioned for.'

She expelled her breath with a sound very much like *phew*, drained half the champagne from her glass and beamed at him. He was puzzled but somewhat relieved, in a tentative sort of way.

'Why are you smiling?' he said.

'I'm not smiling. Go ahead.'

'You were smiling.'

'Was I?'

'Yes. You definitely smiled. This isn't good news, and it'll be even harder for me to say if you're grinning at me.'

'But it's about the film.'

'That's right.'

'Somebody else got the part?' she said. She may not have been smiling now, but she certainly wasn't frowning.

'Not exactly. The thing is, we had this scriptwriter preparing the screenplay, a fairly famous guy, and . . . Well, without going into too much detail, the backers rejected what he came up with, and he got angry, and the week before last he pulled out.'

'Oh. So you have to find someone else to write it?'

'It's not that easy. The distributor agreed to the project on the condition that this particular writer be involved. There was a little nastiness between the backers and the distribution company as a result, and . . . Well, I'm no expert on the movie business, but I know there's no way a film can get made without backing and distribution. Next week they'll announce that production has been temporarily suspended, but I'm afraid the truth is that this project will probably never see the light of day.'

Aoyama glanced at her. She was beaming again. And what she said took him completely by surprise.

'You must be awfully disappointed. But I . . . this is selfish of me, I know, but I'm kind of glad.'

'Glad?'

'I'm sorry. It's terrible of me to say that, after—'

'Why are you glad?'

'Don't you remember what I wrote in that essay? I was 100 per cent certain I wouldn't be chosen for the part. But I knew that if someone else got it, you and she would be spending a lot of time together, and I didn't really relish the thought of that. So, from a strictly selfish point of view . . . Besides, I was afraid the "bad news" might be something else – that you couldn't see me any more, for example, or that we wouldn't be able to meet as often.'

She held her glass up to his again. The delicate rims rang like tiny, perfect bells, and Aoyama felt the tension drain from his shoulders.

8

THE RESTAURANT, ON A back alley in the drinking-and-dining district of East Nakano, would have been all but invisible to the unsuspecting eye: there was no neon, not even a signboard, announcing its existence. He and Ryoko had come here often, and the exterior hadn't changed at all since those days. But foreign streetwalkers and young male hookers with heavy make-up now milled about in the alley, hounding any drunks who stumbled by. They didn't even glance at Aoyama, however, as he passed with Yamasaki Asami on his arm. He noticed her studying a few of them on the walk from the main street, where the taxi had dropped them, but there was no indication of anything like scorn or fear in her expression: she looked at these people as she might look at anyone. As he led her down the alley, carving a path through the prostitutes, he was aware of a certain sense of superiority – not in relation to them, personally, but to their fate. These were unfortunate men and women who were forced to sell their bodies and their pride. He, on the other hand, was with a beautiful young lady, and he was in love. He felt truly blessed.

At the top of the handwritten menu, in brushed ink calligraphy, were the words EDO KURUWA RYORI. It was a small place – seven seats at a counter and two tables. Seated together at one of the tables were the only other customers: three white-haired gentlemen who might have been presidents or directors of banks or trading companies. They were talking about things like golf and the stock market and health issues, and sipping in a refined way at their cups of cold saké. Kai, the owner, was dressed as always in a kimono. She brought steaming hand-towels and a pair of cocktails in faceted Satsuma glasses.

'Hello, stranger,' she said to Aoyama.

Yamasaki Asami tasted her cocktail and gasped.

'That's delicious!' she said.

Her voice reverberated in the small room, and all three of the white-haired gentlemen slowly turned in their elegant tailored suits to look at her. Each was old enough to have seen more than his share of beautiful women, but they must have been struck by something in that uncommon voice of hers. That soft but pene-trating voice that caressed your ears and climbed through your brain like a vine.

'I'm glad you like it,' said Kai with a welcoming smile. 'Speciality of the house – iced saké and citron.'

Kai had been a geisha in Shimbashi. At least ten years older than Aoyama, she'd retired in her mid-thirties to marry a doctor but soon divorced and opened this restaurant. She'd developed an incredible network of patrons over the course of her career, including VIPs in every field from finance to mass media. (He'd once asked who her most memorable customer was, only to be mildly astonished by the answer: Khrushchev.) Aoyama hadn't known her in her geisha days, of course, but he'd been coming here for nearly twenty years. Kai had always liked Ryoko, and Aoyama had never hesitated to talk to her about his private life. He'd been eager for her to meet Yamasaki Asami.

After the introduction, Kai rejoined the gentlemen at their table. Her assistant, a woman on the verge of middle age who was slightly lame in one leg, brought out an appetiser of jellied blowfish. Though it was November, the room was well heated, and she shuffled over the tatami barefoot, as did Kai. There was something strangely alluring, Aoyama thought as he watched her limp back to the kitchen, about a woman in bare feet and full, traditional kimono.

'What is *kuruwa ryori*, exactly?' Yamasaki Asami asked him as she reached for a slice of blowfish with her chopsticks.

'The most common theory,' he said, 'is that it originated with dishes served in the pleasure quarters

123

back in the Edo era, but some say it's actually from the inns on the old Tokaido Road. In any case, it's the epitome of Edo chic, and in my opinion it's much more inviting and likeable than *kaiseki*, for example.'

Sitting with the white-haired old gentlemen, Kai wasn't talking much but keeping their cups full and listening closely to what they had to say. When they directed a question to her ('You don't play any golf, do you, Kai?'), she kept her replies brief and genial ('I can't stand all that walking!'). Lending an ear was as much an art for a woman in her position as it was for bartenders and hostesses. And Kai was a past master.

'I don't even know very much about *kaiseki*,' Yamasaki Asami said.

She seemed somewhat more restrained than she'd been at the French or Italian restaurants they'd gone to. She was probably a bit intimidated by the insular atmosphere of the place, Aoyama thought, remembering that Ryoko too had felt that way at first.

'It would be abnormal to know much about *kaiseki* at your age.'

'But they say it's delicious.'

'I've never really found it all that tasty.'

The assistant brought out yellowtail sashimi, lacquered bowls filled with clams in a broth, and warmed *ginjoshu* saké from Ishikawa prefecture. Yamasaki Asami's nearly translucent cheeks took on a faint blush as she sipped from her cup.

'*Kaiseki*,' Aoyama said, glancing at the elderly gentlemen and lowering his voice mischievously, 'is essentially a cuisine designed for senior citizens.'

She laughed – that laugh like medicine for the ears – and said 'How so?' as she daubed wasabi on a slice of yellowtail.

Aoyama gazed down at her hand manipulating the chopsticks. Her slender fingers, the light pink polish of her fingernails, the blue veins faintly visible on the back of her hand. The skin so smooth it might have been a man-made membrane.

'The common denominator of all *kaiseki* dishes,' he said, 'is the soft texture. None of them make any demands on your teeth. There's no meat to speak of, and even shrimps, for example, are mashed into dumplings. It's all very refined, I suppose, but . . . I don't know, you might say that *kaiseki* is basically about dishes that are easy to chew.'

He'd thought he was somewhat accustomed to being with her now, but sitting side by side like this, brushing shoulders, was making him tense. His throat was dry, and he had to suppress the impulse to drink too quickly. When one is tense, especially around a desirable member of the opposite sex, one tends either to clam up or to talk too much. Aoyama was of the latter persuasion.

'People always talk about the health benefits of Japanese food,' he said, 'but I'm fascinated by other aspects of the Japanese dining experience. Like the whole system of serving food at a counter like this, with the customers all facing the same direction, instead of each other. It's strange when you think about it. At a sushi bar, for example, everyone's facing the *itamae*-san, and you discuss the things you're eating – what type of squid this is, and where they're caught, and how this is the season for them but they'll only be at their best for another couple of weeks, and so on. Discussing the food with the chef even as you eat it – that's a peculiar system.'

'I suppose it is, isn't it? I don't go to sushi restaurants very often – they're so expensive – and I could probably count the number of times I've sat at the counter, but I know what you mean. There's something about that atmosphere.'

'At its worst, it's almost an atmosphere of collusion.'

'Collusion?'

'Everyone at the counter becomes a member of the group. In some sushi bars, *all* the customers are regulars and they all know each other. As an outsider, you need courage to walk into a place like that and take a seat. It's a tight-knit little community, and harmony is of the utmost importance. Nobody's confronting anyone else individually. The conversation all proceeds through the chef, who's like a moderator or a master of ceremonies. You couldn't spend some quiet time with a lover, for example, in a place like that, because you'd be isolating yourselves from the others and spoiling the atmosphere for everyone.'

'I guess that's true.'

'And I'll tell you something else: sushi and *kaiseki* are two foods I never crave when I'm really run-down or stressed.'

'No?'

'When you're overseas, for example, and you're physically tired and your nerves are frazzled, the last thing you want are cold slices of sushi, or all the subtle little tastes of *kaiseki*. At least that's my experience, but I think it's a fairly common one. Different people crave different things, of course, but when I'm feeling exhausted I prefer spicy food like Korean or Sichuan Chinese. Spices stimulate the appetite.'

'I love spicy food. Indian food, for example.'

'Indian food's great, isn't it? Most spicy cuisines originated in hot climates – Cambodia, Thailand, Vietnam, they're all tropical places – but in Korea the climate is relatively cold. I've wondered about that before, why it is that so much Korean food is spicy. Korea has an incredibly rich culture, but history has been cruel to the people. The Koreans have suffered enormously, in very basic and concrete ways – being invaded and occupied by foreigners, having relatives murdered before their eyes, that sort of thing. It's hard for most of us even to imagine what they've been through. But no matter how bad your situation is, you need to eat. And spicy food is a powerful ally when your reserves of courage and energy are low, because it stimulates your appetite. Sushi and *kaiseki* don't have that sort of power. The portions are cold and fresh and bite-size and soft and go down easily, but they aren't foods that lend you strength when you don't have the strength to take sustenance. My theory is that sushi and *kaiseki* are dishes that evolved in peaceful, prosperous times, when eating well was the normal state of affairs. In this country we have the illusion that there's always this warm, loving community we belong to, but the other side of that is a sort of exclusiveness and xenophobia, and our food reflects this. Japanese cuisine isn't inclusive at all – in fact it's extremely inhospitable to outsiders, to people who don't fit into the community.'

As he talked, Aoyama emptied five of the little Mikawachi-yaki cups of warmed *ginjoshu*. Talking too much, he thought, and reminded himself that he'd better ease up – he would be ill-advised to discuss his personal life while drunk. Yamasaki Asami laid down her chopsticks and peered at him. What a beautiful face, he thought, and what a mysterious face. It seemed different from every angle.

'Do you always think about things like this?' she said.

'Like what?'

'The things you were just talking about.'

'Not always, no. I guess it's just a matter of living a long time – the thoughts accumulate, especially the useless ones.'

She helped herself to the last piece of yellowtail sashimi.

'I think you have the most original ideas,' she said. 'I could listen to you for hours.'

Aoyama hoped he wasn't blushing. The barefooted assistant brought another small bottle of warmed saké, along with more starters – grilled eel, steamed *kyoimo* taros, and *shimeji* mushrooms in a black-pepper sauce.

'You may be the first man I've ever gone out with,' Yamasaki Asami said, 'who spoke to me as if I had a brain.'

The three old gentlemen had finished their dessert of dried persimmons, and now Kai was helping them on with their coats. Their amiable conversation continued as they prepared to leave: 'Shall we stop by Ginza?' 'I can't, I'm off for Seattle early tomorrow morning.' 'Those long flights are hard on the immune system, they say, not to mention the lower back.' Passing behind them on the way out, the gentlemen murmured 'Excuse us' and 'Good night', confirming what Aoyama already knew – that those with real power are unfailingly courteous.

'Most men,' Yamasaki Asami continued, 'don't seem to take young women like me seriously.'

'Well, I'm afraid I've been babbling a bit.'

'I think what you were saying was very perceptive. And interesting.'

He took another sip of saké and smiled sheepishly.

'Just talking off the top of my head, really,' he said. 'The truth is, I *love* sushi.'

Yamasaki Asami laughed. Kai was seeing the old gentlemen off, and the assistant was in the back somewhere, so the two of them were alone for a moment. Aoyama laughed too, not because what he'd said was very funny, but because some of the tension had finally evaporated. It was time to broach the subject foremost in his mind. Kai came back in but sat in the far corner of the room and lit a cigarette. She smoked non-filtered Peace.

'I wanted to discuss something else fairly serious tonight,' Aoyama began.

Yamasaki Asami glanced up at him, sensing his nervousness, and immediately set down her chopsticks. Her cheeks were faintly flushed. She folded her hands in her lap and lowered her gaze, listening.

'I haven't told you anything about my private life,' he went on. 'My wife . . . Seven years ago she died of cancer.'

At the word 'wife', Yamasaki Asami tensed up visibly. At the word 'died', she turned to face him.

'I haven't had a real relationship with anyone since her death. Which is not to say I'm some sort of

130

paragon of morality, mind you. But after she died, I just buried myself in my work. I told you about the German pipe organist. Well, it was right after my wife died that I got involved in that project. I used to come to this restaurant with her a lot – but please don't take that the wrong way. It's not that I'm looking for a replacement for my wife, or that you remind me of her, or anything like that. You're a different person, of course, completely different – in fact, I think you're utterly unique. Which is why, as I've come to know you over the past couple of months, I've . . . Well, I've started to think about getting married again.'

He couldn't help noticing that Yamasaki Asami was not taking this well. The rosy flush had drained from her cheeks, and now the shoulders of her glossy black dress were trembling.

'Forgive me if I'm putting you on the spot,' he said. 'I know what a farce this is if you don't feel the same way, but I decided I had to ask anyway. I'm a widower, and I'm tired of being alone. I'd like to continue seeing you, with an eye to getting married eventually.'

She looked up at him, then immediately dropped her gaze. She tried awkwardly to twist her lips into a smile but soon abandoned the effort and shook her head.

'I'm not that sort of person.'

There was something unsettling about her voice as she said this. Aoyama felt as if a cold wind had swept over him. *Not that sort of person.* What did it mean? That she had no intention of being tied down? Or simply that she wasn't taking their relationship as seriously as he was?

'I'm sorry,' she said and stood up. Kai glanced over at them.

Aoyama felt as if his biggest fear had been realised. He knew he had to act but couldn't think of anything to do or say. He sat there paralysed as Yamasaki Asami took her leather coat from the hook on the wall.

'Forgive me,' she said. 'I want to go home now.'

The expression on her face was strangely vacant and frigid, and Aoyama didn't know how to react. All he could do was watch in a kind of daze as she walked out and quietly closed the door behind her. Kai stubbed out her cigarette and said, 'What are you waiting for? Go after her.'

Leather coat in hand, Yamasaki Asami was all but running as she threaded her way through the street-walkers. Aoyama had to sprint if he wanted to catch her before she reached the main street.

'Asami-san!'

He called her name, but his throat was so tight and dry that his shout came out more like a whimper. The streetwalkers' alley seemed surreal to him now. The faces of the ladies in their gaudy clothing and the boys with their thick make-up and bizarre wigs seemed to leap at him in a series of close-ups. He felt as if he'd been thrust into a Fellini film, or a nightmare. A chaos of colours flashed before his eyes – a green bouffant hairdo, metallic silver toenails in purple high heels, the scarlet lipstick of a male hooker, the vivid pink of a pair of lamé stockings. He felt disorientated and had no idea what he was doing, or what he was going to say to her. The cold night air on his face was all that seemed to connect him to reality.

'Asami-san!'

When he yelped her name for the third time, she turned and stopped to wait for him. He got close enough in the dim light to see that her brows were knitted with what looked like annoyance.

'I'm sorry for suddenly blurting out such a thing. It was stupid of me. At least let me help you find a taxi. You can respond to what I said next time, or on the phone if you prefer. Or maybe it's not even something you have to think about, but that's all right too. I just felt I needed to say what I said.'

She shook her head with the same irritated expression and muttered something. He could see her breath in the night air but couldn't hear what she said. The odd sense of being in a movie still hadn't left him. Only the white vapour of his own breath seemed unambiguously real.

She peered up at him as if she were about to speak but then turned, letting her head droop, and slowly continued towards the street. So slowly that it was difficult to keep from outpacing her. Aoyama paused every few steps and gazed blankly at the distant cluster of skyscrapers that loomed over the buildings ahead. Red lights flashed atop them, each blinking at its own regular pace, as if registering a different heartbeat. When they reached the street they stopped and turned to face each other. Neither made any attempt to hail a taxi. She was still carrying her coat. He gently lifted it from her arm and draped it over her shoulders, and as he did so, she teetered forwards and threw her arms around him, burying her face in his neck. Her shoulders were trembling violently, and the embrace was an extremely awkward one. Aoyama was too stunned to know what to do. He held her as if to keep her from falling, the cold leather of her coat slipping under his fingers. Then she let go of him and took a step back.

'You're not just toying with me, are you?' Her voice was an unfamiliar, icy whisper, and her face underwent a sudden and startling transformation as she spoke. It was as if she were shedding some sort of membrane. A wave of goose-pimples rippled over Aoyama's flesh.

'Of course not,' he said hoarsely. 'I've never been more serious.'

He watched her face return to normal. As if that transparent membrane were slowly re-adhering to her skin. It didn't seem like something she was doing consciously – putting on a mask to hide her true self, for example, or to protect herself from the eyes of others – but rather a natural process, a physical response. As natural as laughing when something was funny, or seething over an insult.

'Thank you,' she said, reverting to the voice he knew so well. A taxi pulled up beside them at the kerb, and she climbed inside. 'And thank you for tonight.' Aoyama bent down and kissed her on the cheek, and she turned to look into his eyes. 'I love you,' she whispered, and pressed her mouth against his.

'Same here,' Aoyama said some moments later.

She waved to him from the back seat of the taxi until it melted into the traffic and was gone.

'Where did you meet her?'

When Aoyama got back to the restaurant, Kai was waiting with another bottle of warmed saké and got out her own Arita-yaki cup to help him drink it. He told her about the audition and about Yamasaki Asami's background and responded frankly, if somewhat mechanically, to her questions. To his own ears his voice sounded like that of a child in a state of shock. He still hadn't recovered from that kiss. Yamasaki Asami's lips were cold and soft and sweet, and the moment the kiss was over he'd experienced, along with exhilaration, a bizarre sense of guilt, or shame. It wasn't quite like anything he'd ever known before – a sense of having done something that can never be retracted, or forgiven. It was a bitter, almost painful, sort of feeling, but it was also intoxicating. Just to taste those lips again, Aoyama thought . . .

I'd probably give up everything I own.

Kai sat facing him across the counter, smoking another Peace, and poured them both some saké. Kai was a classic beauty, but right now all Aoyama could see were the lines of age on her face.

'So, what do you think?' he asked, but not in the spirit of actually soliciting her opinion. It was more of an attempt to confirm what he already knew: *She's really something, isn't she? You just don't find young women like her any more. You see that, don't you?*

'Strange girl,' Kai said, exhaling smoke.

'Strange?'

'I've never met a girl quite like that before.'

'Well, it's a whole new generation, Kai.'

'That's true, but some things never change. What's most important to a person, that's the question. Always has been and always will be. When I meet someone, I can usually tell within a minute or two what it is they value most. The young people nowadays – men and women, amateurs and pros – generally fall into one of two categories: either they don't know what it is that's most important to them, or they know but don't have the power to go after it. But this girl's different. She knows what's most important to her and she knows how to get it, but she doesn't let on what it is. I'm pretty sure it's not money, or success, or a normal happy life, or a strong man, or some weird religion, but that's about all I can tell you. She's like smoke: you think you're seeing her clearly enough, but when you reach for her there's nothing there. That's a sort of strength, I suppose. But it makes her hard to figure out.'

'She's nice, though, right?' Aoyama said.

Kai seemed taken aback by this. She shook her head and stubbed out her cigarette.

'Is that really what you think?' she said.

A simple question, but it rocked him. He knew perfectly well that Yamasaki Asami wasn't simply a nice girl, and yet that was how he'd chosen to think of her. Kai had put her finger on this bald self-deception, and he had the odd sensation of wanting to be surprised but not being able to.

'Anyway,' he said, 'I'm sure she's not a bad person. I'm pretty serious about her.'

Kai frowned and shook her head again.

'Nice person, bad person – that's not the level this girl is at. I can see you're crazy about her and probably won't be able to hear this, Ao-chan, but I think you'd be better off staying away from someone like her. I can't read her exactly, but I can tell you she's either a saint or a monster. Maybe both extremes at once, but not somewhere in between.'

137

9

THE NEXT MORNING, AROUND nine-thirty, Yamasaki Asami telephoned the office. It was the first time she'd ever called him.

'Aoyama-san, there's a Miss Yamasaki on line four.'

Takamatsu, a young female staff member, had taken the call. The office was one large room, and Aoyama had no private quarters of his own. His employees called him simply 'Aoyama-san' – with the exception of Tanaka, an accountant in his fifties, who preferred the more conventional 'Chief'. Takamatsu would naturally have asked what the call was in reference to. What had her reply been?

'It's me,' she said when he picked up the phone. 'I'm sorry to bother you at work.'

The staff would hear his side of the conversation – but so what, he thought. He'd eventually have to fill them all in anyway. Marrying a woman who was nearly twenty years younger than himself, and more beautiful than your average film star, was likely to earn him some teasing, but he was sure they'd all be happy for him.

'Is it a bad time?'

'Not at all,' he said. 'I was thinking of calling you anyway.'

'I just couldn't wait any longer to hear your voice.'

'I know. Same here.'

Takamatsu, tapping at her computer keyboard, glanced over at him. Takamatsu was twenty-five. After graduating from college she'd spent a year in London, and upon returning to Japan she'd worked for a small TV station in her home town. But she'd left that job and applied to Aoyama's company because of her burning ambition to work on real documentaries. At her interview she'd come across as fairly impertinent, and the senior staff members had opposed hiring her, but Aoyama was impressed with her English skills and her fire. He put her in charge of licensing foreign documentaries and facilitating joint projects with production companies overseas. Unlike so many young people, she managed to remain both passionate and objective about projects she worked on, not letting her own personal tastes cloud her judgement. Her boyfriend was a foreigner.

'I'm sorry about last night,' Yamasaki Asami said. 'I guess I kind of lost it.'

'There's nothing to apologise for. It was my fault for bringing up something like that out of the blue.'

'Do you understand why I'm calling?'

'I think so. I wanted to hear your voice too.'

There was a subtle difference in the way she spoke to him now. Polite and refined as always, but she was using somewhat less formal language, and her voice seemed somehow more intimate, more trusting. That, Aoyama realised, was a direct result of last night's kiss, and the fact that they now shared a secret of sorts. Aoyama welcomed this change, of course, and he found her voice more bewitching than ever. He had to concentrate to keep from breaking into a goofy smile.

'I still don't completely understand,' she said. 'Or, rather, I still don't completely believe it.'

'What I said last night?'

'Of course. What else?'

'It was all so sudden, after all.'

'But it's true . . . isn't it?'

'It's true. Everything I said last night is the truth.'

He hadn't got around to telling her about Shige, but that wasn't a lie. Hearing her voice, he wished he could see her, be with her. And once that thought had occurred to him, every nerve in his body seemed to crackle with desire.

'Can we meet again soon?' she asked.

'Of course. I wish it could be right now.'

He told her he'd call back later in the day to arrange something.

Takamatsu was watching him and smiled when he ended the call. He wondered if he should confide in her, ask her advice. He didn't know what his next step with Yamasaki Asami should be. There was the question of sex, for example. Having confirmed their mutual feelings with that kiss, should they nonetheless wait until they were married to make love? He had hinted at this question to Kai the night before.

'Should you sleep with her?' Kai had said. 'You got me. Young women today are all over the map on that one. Some are offended if men try to have sex with them and some are offended if they don't. So I have no way of knowing, particularly when it comes to a girl who's so hard to read. But one thing I can say for sure is that the more intimate you become with her, the more obsessed you're going to get. You've got to carve it into your skull, Ao-chan, that you don't really know anything about this girl. And it's not as if there's some infallible method for getting at the truth. You know, there's something old-school about this one, in a way. Back in the day, in the geisha world, you'd run across a girl kind of like her every now and then. Breathtakingly beautiful, very popular with the clients, nothing but the top class of patrons, but basically unfathomable. They'd have an almost unnatural sort of beauty, the sort of beauty that made you wonder if it hadn't been nourished by all the misery and misfortune in the world. The sort of beauty that can destroy a man. And of course that sense of danger, too, seems to drive men wild. The old *femme fatale* thing.'

Aoyama invited Takamatsu out to lunch. He phoned from the office to reserve a table at what she said was her favourite restaurant in Tokyo, an Indian place in Jingu-mae. There were only eight tables, and people without reservations were queuing. Takamatsu was a regular, apparently: the head waiter knew her and seated them next to a window with a view of the Jingu woods.

'Shall we have beer?' she suggested.

Aoyama ordered two bottles of Indian brew. Takamatsu drank hers straight from the bottle, the label of which featured three pink flamingoes. He waited until the tandoori chicken and prawns arrived before relating the story thus far, from his first meeting with Yamasaki Asami to last night's kiss.

When he finished, Takamatsu said, 'Good heavens. When did you become such a romantic?'

'Me?'

'Uh-huh.'

'I've become a romantic?'

'Could there be a more classic case? Aoyama-san, I always thought of you as one of the few people in Japan who's capable of making a proper documentary.'

'What's that got to do with it?'

'You're the one who taught me that romance has no place in documentaries – not as a motivating force,

142

anyway. That it's too amorphous and vague and ultimately insidious.'

'I said that?'

'Not in so many words, maybe, but it's one of the things I've learned from you. Naturally work and private life are two different things – I'm basically a romantic myself, I'd say – but it's never good to let romance blind you to the truth, is it?'

The silhouetted branches of plane trees waved in the wind outside the window. A dish of aubergine and shredded meat was placed before them, and Aoyama studied Takamatsu's face as she dug in. He felt he finally understood what Kai had been saying the night before. Takamatsu had an average face. She was attractive enough – bursting with confidence and ambition and blessed with regular features and a good grasp of make-up and fashion. Quite sexy, really, but average none-theless. Yamasaki Asami's face and body, on the other hand, evoked a kind of perilous fragility that made you feel as if things were on the verge of collapse, as if the centre couldn't hold and the axis had already begun to tilt. When he was around her, he was in a constant state of mild anxiety. His heartbeat would speed up, and he was never truly at ease.

'So there's something I'm missing?' he said.

'Duh!'

'But I'm perfectly aware that I'm crazy about her. Doesn't that count for anything?'

'Do you want to have sex with her?'

He hesitated before answering that. If he replied truthfully – *Of course, but I have this fear that she'll vanish at the first touch* – Takamatsu was sure to laugh. Suddenly he felt as if he understood what 'romantic' meant.

'Sure I do.'

'Why haven't you, then?'

He nodded but said nothing, staring at his spoonful of pork curry.

'You're afraid to, right?' Takamatsu was wearing a thoughtful frown, but when Aoyama nodded again she laughed. He laughed too. 'Good heavens!' she said.

'It's not that I'm afraid the sex won't go well,' he hastened to explain.

'Let's hope not. Any man over forty who's still bad in bed might as well stop breathing.'

'So, what *am* I afraid of? That something would go wrong and she'd stop liking me?'

'You're asking yourself that one, right?'

'Yeah. I guess I'm just so nuts about her that . . . I don't know. It's not as if there's anything specific to be afraid of. I'm just afraid.'

'That's the romanticism.'

'Yeah, well, whatever it is, it's self-indulgent and counter-productive. And it's not as if I don't know any of the lines men use to try and seduce women. Why not just pick one, and if she turns me down she turns me down and we wait till we're married? Simple enough, right?'

They were enjoying a dessert made of carrots and milk when Takamatsu said, 'So where would you go to have sex? A hotel? Or your house in Suginami?'

'Maybe I'll take her away somewhere for a weekend.'

She nodded. 'Not a bad idea.'

'That's right. We're installing a new computer system, so I'm going to close down the office for a couple of days while they set it up. Anyway, there's this great hotel in Izu, fantastic food, hot springs, the works. I thought it would be nice to get away and have a chance to really talk about things. Do you think you'd be interested?'

After returning from lunch, Aoyama had stepped out to a pay phone. Yamasaki Asami's response was immediate and enthusiastic. 'I'd love to!' she said in her most animated voice. Aoyama was tense from just pronouncing words like 'hotel' and 'hot springs'. It was, he thought, very much like saying, 'Let's not wait till we're married to have sex.' There were no official guidelines for seducing a woman, or for analysing her response. But at some point, as a man, you had to make a move.

'What sort of clothing should I bring?'

'Clothing?'

'I suppose people dress fairly formally in a place like that?'

'Not at all. It's a resort, so casual is fine.'

Before ending the call he arranged a time and place to meet but didn't raise the question of one room or two. In fact, he'd already reserved the room just before calling her: a junior suite with twin beds. They'd leave on Saturday, three days from now.

He needed to tell Shige about this, of course, and did so at dinner that evening. Shige had no objections but admitted to wishing he could have met her first.

'Just one night?' he asked.

'Yeah. I'll be home by Sunday evening.'

'You're not eloping, are you?'

'Very funny. I just want to spend some time alone with her, to make sure of her feelings, before introducing you. Pretty awkward to have you meet her and then find out she's not looking to get married after all.'

'Don't take this the wrong way, Pops, but . . .'

'What?'

'Have you told her that she won't exactly be leading a life of luxury? That there's no family fortune to speak of? That you don't own this house, for example, or that your car is Made in Japan instead of being a Mercedes or something?'

'Not in so many words, no. What – you think she's after me for my money?'

'Nah. I think even you would be able to see through somebody that shallow. But it's possible she might have this vague idea that you're rich, right? It's important to be clear about things like that.'

'You're right. I'll make sure we have that discussion during the trip.'

'I think you should, Pops. You have a tendency to come off as sort of a rich guy sometimes.'

Shige said he'd invite a friend to stay over Saturday night, and that he'd explain the situation to Rie-san.

'I bet she'll be surprised,' he said.

The hotel, about an hour's drive past the city of Ito, was connected to a championship golf course. A major tournament was held there each spring, and through summer and into autumn the place was always full. In winter, however, reservations were easy to come by.

They didn't talk much during the drive. But anticipation hung like a haze in the climate-controlled atmosphere of the car. As they flew along the motorway with their sunglasses on and their bags in the trunk, it was as if the tension of desire were a tangible force in the narrow space between them. Aoyama barely even noticed the scenery. Yamasaki Asami had brought a flask full of coffee, and on the way, between brief bouts of small talk, he drank three cups. He'd decided to hold off on the serious discussions until they were alone in the room. They'd be spending an uprecedentedly long time alone, after all, a whole night together.

The hotel stood at the tip of a promontory overlooking the Izu seashore. Its orange roof had appeared suddenly as they rounded a curve in the descending road, and then the building itself, which wouldn't have looked out of place in the south of France. The long, winding driveway, the immaculate landscaping and flowerbeds, the courteous service of the doorman and bellboys, and the spaciousness and warmth of the lobby, with its oversized leather sofas, all seemed to make quite an impression on Yamasaki Asami. 'It's fantastic,' she murmured as they strolled to the front desk. Now that he thought about it, ever since their first meeting he'd taken her nowhere but the finest restaurants and bars he knew of. And now this. *She might have this vague idea that you're rich, right?* Shige had said. Pretty perceptive, Aoyama thought, for a high-school kid. Or should he make that: *because* he was a high-school kid?

She stood close to him, looking up at the high ceilings and the huge Spanish-style wrought-iron chandelier, as he filled out the registration card. Putting her name down as 'Aoyama Asami', he wondered if the excitement he was feeling didn't somehow contradict his dream of establishing a new life, a new little family.

There was a small balcony attached to the suite, from which you could see the golf course and the sea.

'So,' Aoyama said, sinking back on the sofa, 'what shall we do till dinner?'

There was a lot they needed to talk about – most pressingly the subject of Shige. But it would be just as well, he thought, to discuss such things at leisure, over dinner. It was now past three in the afternoon. The sun would be going down in an hour or so. There was no dearth of possible activities, but it was too early for some and too late for others. She sat down right next to him. Red leather pumps, pale beige trousers, red sweater, beige scarf, hair tied back artlessly. Her knee was pressed lightly against his. She put her sunglasses on, then took them off again and peered up at him.

'There's a small museum,' he said, 'about twenty or thirty minutes from here. Mostly Japanese paintings, but a decent collection of impressionists too. If we leave now, I think we can get in well before closing time. Or, let's see . . . There's a fishing port over that way, behind the hotel, that's kind of fun. A little port with a few beat-up old fishing boats and a café overlooking the docks. They serve the most incredibly delicious coffee there . . .'

She set her sunglasses down on the coffee-table and undid her hair. It cascaded to her shoulders in slow motion, and Aoyama became conscious of a certain indefinable fragrance. Her shampoo, or some other hair product, maybe. Or perfume. Or maybe, he thought, it wasn't a fragrance at all, but some other

149

force washing over his senses and expanding to fill the darkening room. Something dense and powerful and chilling.

'The owner of this café is an interesting guy. He used to be a boxer, and he loves movies and literature, so the place is full of books and film magazines and whatnot. Nothing quite like a fishing port at dusk.'

She wasn't listening. She removed her scarf, folded it neatly, and set it down on the arm of the sofa. The heat was on, and Aoyama was beginning to perspire beneath his sweater. She stood up and walked to the entryway, where she turned off all the lights in the room. The shadows of evening rushed in, and he was aware of the fragrance, or whatever it was, growing thicker and heavier, like wine fermenting. He didn't know what to do. He felt completely at her mercy, and was unable even to ask why she'd turned out the lights. It was getting harder to breathe, but he continued blathering on.

'I know! Let's go to the baths. They have these huge hot-spring pools. You get to them through the golfers' changing rooms, but they're open to all the guests, not just golfers. And as I recall there's a sauna, too – or is it a Jacuzzi? Anyway, we could soak in the baths awhile, then play billiards afterwards. Or table tennis, they have that too. Or we could always have a cocktail at the bar . . .'

The last of the sunlight was slowly bleeding over the floor at his feet, and now she was standing in the semi-darkness between the twin beds, undressing. Her face was in shadow, but as she peeled off her clothing, slowly revealing her back and shoulders, her neck and arms, her thighs and knees, she seemed to be either grinning or scowling. When she stepped out of her panties and got into bed, Aoyama sputtered and ran out of mindless drivel.

'Please,' she said. 'Come here.' There was nothing tender or submissive about the way she said this. Her voice was urgent and intense, almost like a cry for help.

'Don't take off your clothes yet. Come over here first. Hurry.'

Aoyama got up and wobbled towards the bed. It felt as if all the oxygen had been sucked out of the room, or as if someone had wallpapered his tongue and throat. When he reached the bedside, she flung back the covers, exposing everything.

'Look,' she said, gazing sadly up at him. 'See these burn scars? My mother's husband did that to punish me.'

She pointed at two small, almost parallel lines that puckered the skin of her left thigh. Aoyama swallowed. He could see the two scars, but no other marks whatsoever. Right before his eyes were her face and neck, her breasts and nipples, her waist, her navel, her pubic hair, and the exquisite curves of her naked legs. Her body was like an idealised abstraction, a porcelain figure.

'Did you see?' she said.

Aoyama nodded robotically.

'Everything?'

He nodded again. He was seized with alternating, contradictory impulses. One was to flee the room, the other to bend down and kiss those flawless breasts that softly rose and fell with her breathing.

'Lie down beside me, then. No, don't undress yet. Lie down beside me with your clothes on.'

Aoyama followed her instructions. He lay down at her side in his sweater and trousers, without even kicking off his shoes. She turned towards him. He pillowed her head with his left arm, and she clung to him and hooked one leg over his.

'You saw everything, right?' she whispered in his ear. 'Did you notice my feet?'

Uh-huh.

Her breast pressed against his sternum, and each thump of his pounding heart caused it to jiggle perceptibly.

'You saw them? What do they look like?'

The toenails are cracked.

'They got that way from ballet.'

I thought so.

'I'm the only one, right?'

Of course.

'Do you understand? You've got to love only me.'

I know.

'Everyone says that, but they don't really mean it. You're different from everyone else, though, aren't you? Only me. I'll give you everything, but I've got to be the only one you love. Do you understand?'

Only me, she kept repeating, only me, as she began to undress him.

10

SHE PULLED HIS SWEATER up and unbuttoned his shirt
with those deft, slender fingers. He watched dumbly as
one button after another came loose. The room was
darkening rapidly, and her pink nail polish faintly
reflected the pale winter sunset. At some point they'd
both sat up on the bed, though he couldn't have said
when. Her downward-tilted face was right before his
eyes. Something about her profile stirred a memory in
him, but it was a memory that never quite materialised. Her cheeks were flushed. Her breasts had filled
out as she sat up, and the size and shape of them, in
proportion to her narrow waist, seemed too perfect to
be real. It was, he thought, as if a sculptor from some
other world had found a way to imbue his work with
softness and moisture and warmth and bring it to life.

Time seemed to be flying by at many times its
normal speed, and then again it seemed to have
stopped completely. She slid her hand inside his shirt
and explored the skin of his chest with plaintive,

quivering fingertips, like a blind person reading a long-awaited letter. Her touch was like a gleaming scalpel slicing open his breast, and then again like the miraculous, gentle touch of a healer. He couldn't distinguish the border between his body and the outside world and was aware only of the points where her fingertips touched his skin, and of the hitherto unimaginable sensations emanating from those points. Her fingertips were like ice, and then again like molten lava. He found himself standing between the two beds with his sweater in his hands but no memory of having stood up or removed it. His shirt was completely unbuttoned, exposing his chest and stomach. Yamasaki Asami undid his belt, then plucked gently at his zip and slowly pulled it down, like a surgeon opening an incision. She was sitting, knees together, on the edge of the bed. He had the dizzying illusion that the green velvet bedspread, illuminated by the white porcelain lamp of her naked body, had billowed out to cover the entire room. Once she'd lowered his zip all the way, she looked up at him, and he felt his pulse throb in his temples. She peered into his eyes and smiled. Then she reached out to press her pink fingernails into his chest and dragged them downwards in a lingering, catlike scratch. He had to stifle a cry. Shameful sounds – a sob, a moan, a sigh – stuck in his throat and threatened to seep out between his lips. Why, he wondered, wasn't he taking control? Why

155

wasn't he pushing her down on the bed and climbing on top of her? He was just standing there with his arms dangling uselessly at his sides, twitching involuntarily in response to the stimulus of her touch. Where had she learned such technique? Were moves like this in the repertoire of all young women these days? Or was it only because of her stunning beauty, and the intensity of his desire for her, that her touch seemed so excruciatingly sensual? When she'd stripped him of his pants and shorts, her eyes seemed to lose focus and her lips parted to reveal the somewhat pointed tip of her tongue. It was as if a pink thorn were sprouting from her face. This tender, wet thorn traced a line down from his navel to his thigh, then back up towards his chest. She got on her knees on top of the bed and lifted her face towards his. He bent down to take her tongue in his mouth. She kissed him hungrily, grabbing his left hand and pressing it against her breast. He closed his eyes to savour the feel of her flesh – she wasn't porcelain after all but unbelievably soft and human and warm and female. He moved his hand down to cup the tuft of her pubic hair. She was wet down there, and hot, and she moaned in a voice unlike anything he'd ever heard before – a hard, deep, metallic voice, like rusted gears groaning into motion.

Aoyama was asleep, and in his dream he was being tortured by persons unknown. After a brief interval of terrifying silence and darkness, a red-hot poker was suddenly in his face. He cried out, opening his eyes wide with terror, but the light was so intense that he immediately closed them again. He was utterly disorientated. He moved his lips, trying to ask what was happening, but the mucous membranes of his throat felt like cobwebs, dry and sticky, and no sound emerged. The insides of his eyelids glowed orange and his optical nerves spasmed with pain. He was utterly devoid of strength. His head felt numb, especially at the temples, and all his senses seemed anaesthetised. What in the world was going on? And where was he? He was lying on a strange bed, uncovered and apparently unclothed. His right hand was down by his hip, his left resting on his stomach.

Whose bed was this?

The light fixture he'd glimpsed above him, on the ceiling, was unfamiliar. Maybe, he thought for a moment, he was still dreaming. But the numbness in his temples and the pain behind his eyes said no, it wasn't a dream. Then he remembered. He was in the hotel room he'd come to with *her*. He reached out with his left hand, but no one was there. Gritting his teeth, he opened his eyes once more, but when the light flooded in he reflexively squeezed them shut again. He'd have to open them little by little. He let the lids ease to a slit and peered through quivering lashes wet with tears that blurred his field of vision. His pulse was irregular and weak, but it began to speed up as he gradually opened his eyes and a certain fact crystallised in his mind.

She was gone.

The room was as brightly lit as a convenience store but absolutely silent, with no hint of another's presence. Aoyama was naked, his shrunken penis hanging limp and matted with strands of semen-caked pubic hair. He listened carefully for signs of someone using the bathroom or taking a shower, but there were none. Perhaps, seeing how soundly he was sleeping, she'd decided to let him rest and gone down to the bar or dining room on her own . . . But no. Her travel bag was gone. Yamasaki Asami had vanished.

His body felt impossibly heavy and sluggish, as if his veins coursed with mercury. His right hand brushed against something hard – his wristwatch, wedged between folds of the bedspread. He snagged it and held it up before his eyes. It was a little past three, and the date had advanced a day. Caught in the steel band was a long hair. Hers.

She had been here in this room with him. There could be no doubt about that.

Aoyama wound the hair around his finger. He was conscious of two different strands of memory. One was in the form of vivid flashbacks: her face, beaded with perspiration. Her pink tongue. Tangled, sweat-soaked hair plastered to her forehead and cheeks. Her

158

tumescent nipples. And her wet, slick crevice oozing a cloudy white secretion as it parted to receive his member. Along with the flashbacks were sounds: sighs and moans, squeals and whispers . . .

The second strand of memory unreeled bit by bit, falteringly. There had been a conversation. He'd told her about Shige. But was that before they'd started having sex or after? Before her first orgasm, or after she'd cried out and clung to him desperately any number of times? He wasn't sure, but he knew that at some point he'd told her about Shige. How had she reacted? He couldn't remember.

What in the name of heaven had happened here? He didn't even remember ejaculating. He reached down and felt his penis. His semen and her fluids had dried to crusty patches on his skin. He remembered her gripping his erection and stroking it. And saying something just before she took him in her mouth. She'd been holding him in her right hand, stimulating him with the fingernails of her left, and she'd said something and then begun using her tongue and lips. Was that before or after he'd told her about Shige?

He rolled on to his side, placed his right palm on the bedspread, and tried to push himself up. Pain shot through his temples and his chest, and he abandoned the effort and flopped face-down on the bed, grimacing. He was breathing hard, his heartbeat was racing, and his torso was so heavy and so devoid of sensation it might have been made of stone. She must have done something to him.

The thought shocked him, but it was nothing compared to the shock of finding her gone. A faint fragrance clung to the bedspread – the same fragrance he'd noticed when she undid her hair. The green bedspread had absorbed the smells of her cologne and make-up and sweat and secretions, but that one fragrance alone held sway over his numbed senses. Flashbacks of rapturous sex continued to flicker in his mind, and with each one he slipped deeper into the fear that he'd lost her for ever. The intervals between the flashbacks gradually diminished, and two images began to predominate: her face and her vagina. Each time he'd thrust his organ deeply into her, her face had distorted. But even with her brow furrowed into a mass of wrinkles, or her eyes wide and unfocused, or her jaw going slack and her tongue lolling out, her features never lost their beauty. And nothing in this world ever looked more deliciously lascivious than that vagina of hers, every wrinkle and fold of which was wet with the juice that issued forth endlessly, sluicing down the trough between her buttocks and dripping to the velvet bedspread. From time to time, when her moans turned to orgasmic squeals, Aoyama had pulled out to lift her to the next level of anticipation and pleasure. Each time he did so, the squeals turned to something like sobs. The small hole in the pink that peeked out between the lips of her vagina would remain open at those times, the white, milky fluid oozing out of it like some primitive, crawling thing. But even then her face had maintained an unimpeachable beauty, and the disconnect between that face and her hungry, lust-crazed pussy had only excited him all the more. That dark pink slit, surrounded by the white flesh of her inner thighs, was the doorway to her inner temple, and assailing it gave Aoyama a taste of cruel and infinitely salacious delight. He had no idea how long the sex had lasted, but he remembered feeling as if it might never end; he'd remained erect and rock-hard until it was actually painful, the skin of his penis stretched so thin it seemed on the verge of splitting open. Now, with his senses dulled and the alternating images of her face and vagina flaring in his brain, the thought that such pleasures might be lost to him for ever was more than he could bear. *Gone.* A chill ran through him, and he began to gag, as if something were stuck in his throat. He didn't want to cry – somehow he felt that tears would mark the end – and was repressing the impulse, biting his lip, when the phone rang. He jerked involuntarily, then clawed his way across the bed to the instrument.

'Mr Aoyama?' It was a man's voice. Aoyama's disappointment drained him of any strength he'd mustered. He'd hoped to hear *her* voice: *It's me.*

Thank goodness you're still there! I was afraid you might have left . . .

'This is the front desk. Is that Mr Aoyama?'

'Yes,' he managed to reply in a miserable croak. 'Yes, this is Aoyama.'

'Forgive me if you were sleeping, sir. We called several times earlier but there was no answer, so we thought it best to keep trying in spite of the hour. When Mrs Aoyama left, we—'

'What time?'

'It's a little past three-thirty a.m.'

'No. What time did she leave?'

'Sir?'

Aoyama explained that he'd taken some cold medicine and fallen asleep.

'She dined alone, sir, and called for a car at about eight o'clock, saying she had urgent business in Tokyo.'

Struggling with the irregular thumping of his heart and the rising nausea, Aoyama said yes, that was right, something had come up.

'Shall I send the hotel doctor up to see you, sir?'

'No, I'll be all right.'

'Please feel free to let us know, sir, if you need anything at all. And . . . May I ask if you're still planning to check out tomorrow? We do need to confirm that.'

'I should be fine after a good night's sleep.'

'Very well, sir. Terribly sorry to bother you. Good night.'

Aoyama hung up the phone and lay there at the edge of the bed. He was not feeling at all well. A cold sweat rolled down his temples and jaw and dripped to the bedspread, but it didn't feel as if it could possibly be his own perspiration, and he actually looked up to see if the ceiling were leaking. He wiped his temples with the back of his hand, and then he checked his pulse. It felt weak again, slow and gurgly. Something bitter was working its way up from his stomach, and he swallowed hard, to try and hold it down. *Sleeping tablets*, he thought suddenly. A large dose. He'd been drugged into unconsciousness and then awakened by his own jangled nerves. He wondered if he should try regurgitating but decided there was no point – too much time had passed. By now the medicine had all been digested and delivered to the capillaries in the farthest reaches of his body.

She had fed him sleeping tablets, he was sure of it.

Several times during the evening, he remembered, she'd torn herself away from him and slipped into the bathroom. He'd thought nothing of it at the time. He knew that prolonged stimulation of the clitoris could cause a woman to pee a lot, and they'd both thirstily guzzled drinks from the minibar as well – beer, cola, whisky. He'd also drunk directly from her mouth. Straddling him, riding him with the motion of her hips, she'd taken mouthfuls of whisky or beer and then transferred them to his mouth with kisses. He remembered squeezing the perfect white globes of her ass as they kissed: he wouldn't have noticed if she'd slipped him sulphuric acid that way, let alone powdered sleeping tablets.

He propped himself up on one elbow and looked at the telephone. Next to it was a memo pad, and something was written on the top sheet, in an almost childish scrawl.

No forgiveness for lies
—The Woman Who Lost Her Name

Lies? Aoyama was puzzled momentarily, and then somewhat relieved – obviously she'd misunderstood something he said. He reached for the phone and dialled her number. No one answered. He tried several more times before giving up, but by then he was feeling much better.

She was a pure and innocent but spirited girl. She'd taken something the wrong way and got angry and left. Wanting to avoid a confrontation, she'd slipped him some of her own sleeping tablets so she could leave without having to explain. She would have brought sleeping tablets, he reasoned, because she was nervous and excited about their first trip together and afraid she wouldn't be able to sleep.

He'd call her tomorrow afternoon and resolve everything; she'd probably end up apologising.

For now it was best to get some sleep. He fumbled with the controls on the side-table, setting the alarm for shortly before checkout time and turning off all the lights, then crawled under the covers. A powerful undercurrent immediately began dragging him down, and sleep washed over him like surf. Just before succumbing, while still on the border of consciousness, he had a very strange sort of dream.

In a small, shabby room a man of fifty or so sits on worn tatami mats. He's dressed in long underwear and drinking. He holds a large bottle of cheap whisky on his knee and pours it into a glass that's cloudy with fingerprints. The man drinks the whisky slowly and takes deep drags on a cigarette. He has no feet. The stubs of his ankles protrude from his long underwear like the ends of oversized sausages. The only thing visible from the room's one small window is the outer wall of the building next door. Gnats are bouncing against a fluorescent light above the table, and one of them has fallen into the man's glass. Furious that he can't stand up and chase the gnats away, he lets out a drunken bellow.

Separated from this room by a torn paper screen is an even smaller room with no windows at all. Inside, in the shadows, a little girl is putting on a pair of ballet shoes. The shoes are worn out, scuffed and torn and no longer pink but a sooty flesh-tone. Once they're snugly on her feet, she stands up. It's summer, and she opens the paper screen slightly to let in a little air. Beads of sweat dot her forehead. What little breeze there is carries the smell of whisky and cigarette smoke – his smell – mixed with an odour of rotting vegetables.

As she's adjusting the screen, the man's expression undergoes a change. His eyes were wild with rage just moments ago, as he grumbled and shouted at the gnats, but now he looks desperate and craven, like a condemned criminal begging for his life. He sets his glass down and glances nervously around behind him, then tries to peer through the partly open doorway. The girl's silhouette flits past the opening as she crosses the dark little room. Her small, slender hands; her undeveloped chest and hips; her lissome legs, glistening with sweat.

The girl knows that the man is watching her and takes care not to give him more than brief glimpses through the opening. He peers down at the stubs of his legs for a moment, then inserts his right hand into his waistband. She's practising the few simple steps she's mastered, her head tilted at an angle that best emphasises the beauty of her face, as she's been taught to do at ballet school. She knows what the man is doing with his right hand, and she's seen the thing he's holding. He's been doing this almost every night for the past few weeks, whenever she practises. He doesn't yell at her any more when she's dancing, or call her names. Instead he gets drunk and watches her out of the corner of his eye, fumbling in his underwear and looking as if he's about to burst into tears. When she senses him moving that hand and making that face, as if begging for mercy, something evaporates from her body, and something else enters to replace it – something dark and indelible . . .

'I don't know what to do. I can't get her on the phone, and I realise now that I don't even know her address.'

Two weeks had passed since the trip to Izu. Aoyama had managed to continue working somehow, and to spend time with Shige, but Yoshikawa was the only one he could really discuss this with. He was calling from a public phone.

'She doesn't answer?'

'It's worse than that. I get a recording saying the number's no longer in service. It's been that way since a few days after Izu.'

'What happened there, exactly?'

'Only what I just told you.'

'But why would she suddenly vanish?'

'I don't know. She must've misunderstood something I said or did. I'm sure we could clear it all up in about two minutes, but I have no way of getting in touch with her.'

167

Yoshikawa was silent for a moment. Then, in a quiet voice, he said, 'You should just let it go.'

Aoyama wanted to smash the receiver against the glass wall of the phone booth. He was literally trembling with rage and exasperation. Since Yamasaki Asami's disappearance he hadn't been able even to eat properly, and his nerves were like live, sizzling wires.

'I know you're not going to listen to anything I tell you,' Yoshikawa said, 'but I'm partly responsible, and I have to say this: I think you should forget about her.'

'You don't get it, Yoshikawa. It was just a little misunderstanding, dammit. I need to find her, and all I'm asking is if you have any ideas. She said she was living in Nakameguro, and I thought you might know the address.'

'Look, the only address I ever saw was the one on the résumé, the one in Suginami, and somebody else lives there now. I told you that before, right? I don't know anything about Nakameguro. Besides, we've already tossed all the résumés . . . Hello? You still there?'

'Yeah. All right. Later,' Aoyama said and hung up the phone.

11

THE NEW YEAR ARRIVED without any word from her. Aoyama had been showing up at work every day, and he tried hard to be himself around Shige in spite of the emotional torture he was going through. But he couldn't hide the physical toll it was taking.

In the two months since Izu he'd lost six kilos. Not even when Ryoko died had he ever found himself in such a state that he couldn't get food down. Ryoko's death, devastating though it was, had been gradual. Seeing her weaken day by day was agonising, but it had given him time to assimilate and process what was happening. To this day he remembered with gratitude the courage Ryoko had shown in those final days. Her gentle resignation in the face of such pain and fear had been a wonderful parting gift to those who loved her.

But Yamasaki Asami had disappeared suddenly. Without any warning or foreshadowing whatsoever – they hadn't even argued or exchanged bitter words – she'd vanished from the hotel room and seemingly from the face of the earth. It was all just some sort of misunderstanding: he still believed this, and that belief was one of the things impeding his recovery. He'd revisited Nakameguro any number of times in the past two months. Starting at the big intersection where the taxi had dropped her off after some of their dates, he'd wandered aimlessly through the maze of side streets. He was fully aware of how pathetic this was and didn't really expect to find her there, but it was all he could think of to do. Nakameguro was the only thread he had left to cling to.

No forgiveness for lies.

He still didn't know what she'd meant by that. All his memories of her were ambrosial and poisonous, in equal measure. He remembered with brutal clarity every detail of every date, to say nothing of those last, ecstatic hours in Izu. And beautiful memories, he'd come to realise, were the sledgehammers of despair.

He'd had dozens of telephone conversations with Yoshikawa, and met with him several times for dinner or drinks. And he'd even discussed the situation with Takamatsu and other members of his staff. But the discussions were usually more about baring his soul and bemoaning his loss than soliciting comfort or advice, and eventually even Yoshikawa tired of hearing it.

I mean, how crazy is this, Yoshikawa? I didn't do anything! Nothing I know of anyway, and up till then everything had been going so well! It would be ridiculous to end it like this . . .

Shige, on the other hand, was a rock. Aoyama wondered how it was possible for a boy his age to have such a firm grasp of this sort of situation. Shige seemed to realise that the worst thing you can do for someone in psychological distress is to give them special treatment. He acted as always towards his father and never once asked about Yamasaki Asami. And when Rie-san rather too persistently expressed concern for Aoyama's health, Shige covered for him, saying, 'Sometimes a man just doesn't feel like eating.' He'd learned about loss when his mother died, and he knew things that Aoyama himself had apparently been forgetting: that pouring your heart out to someone affords only temporary relief at best; that you just have to resign yourself to a period of suffering, somehow going about your everyday business as you slowly find a way to assimilate the loss.

Damned impressive for a sixteen-year-old, thought Aoyama. He was sitting on the living-room sofa, with his bare feet up on the coffee-table, eating yogurt. It was the last Sunday of January. Shige had left early that morning to go skiing with a friend, saying he probably wouldn't be home till late but not to wait up. Gangsta was outside, barking as usual. Born to hunt, the beagle was big on vocalising. He'd howl along with ambulance sirens, bay at sparrows and crows, and sometimes even yelp at insects crawling over the ground.

Aoyama had walked to a nearby market earlier to purchase the yogurt, along with salmon roe in soy sauce, deep-fried tofu and cabbage rolls. He had no appetite whatsoever, and food still turned to ashes in his mouth, but he knew he had to maintain at least the will to get back on his feet, if only for Shige's sake. Two things were necessary, he believed, in order to maintain that will: work he could get motivated about, and proper nourishment. He couldn't spend the rest of his life showing Shige how weak and pathetic he was.

He mixed some honey into the yogurt and sat there on the sofa forcing himself to eat it. Even something as soft and mild as yogurt was difficult to swallow. It wasn't that his system was actively rejecting food, but as if the nerves were too busy retracing memories of Yamasaki Asami to send out signals demanding nourishment. He'd only been with her once, yet images of her naked breasts and sex, her hips and fingertips, streamed incessantly through his mind. He'd look at a top nude model in some magazine, and his entire nervous system would insist that there was no comparison. It was like a narcotic, he thought, and not just metaphorically. Her voice and smell and touch had provided him with exactly the same sort of thing, chemically speaking, that certain drugs provide, and the receptors in his brain were clamouring for her.

There was nothing else that could take her place, as far as his nervous system was concerned. The nerves were honest, and strictly physiological. Reasoning didn't work with them.

He was listening to music as he ate the yogurt. With his nerves as battered as they were, it had become painfully clear to him how irritating television can be. *You may be feeling like shit*, the TV screams at you, *but the rest of the world is carrying on just fine!* He'd begun listening to a lot of classical music – from Bach to Debussy, from gloomy, minor-key symphonies to lighthearted piano pieces. Nothing was less abrasive or helped the time to pass better than classical music. A single Mozart piano concerto lasted about thirty minutes, for example, and listening to Nos. 20 to 27 ate up four whole hours. Of course, not even the magic of Barenboim's piano could obliterate the unbearably evocative image of Yamasaki Asami, and not even Mozart could neutralise the suffering. But the beauty of the melodies and arrangements was soothing to the nerves, and if he just sat drinking in that beauty, the second hand on his watch would continue its leisurely sweep, and eventually night would arrive. Then he could reach for the cognac or whisky.

He forbade himself spirits during the daytime. He'd realised within a couple weeks of Yamasaki Asami's disappearance that alcohol was no way to deal with the agony. Several hungover mornings, after too little sleep, Aoyama had experienced an almost debilitating sense of self-loathing, seeing himself as a total failure in life. Deep grief was like a physical wound, and too much alcohol only impaired the healing process.

What he was drinking with his yogurt at two in the afternoon on this Sunday, therefore, was a cup of Fortnum & Mason apple tea. The music was a collection of Verdi overtures. Playing right now was Von Karajan conducting *La Forza del Destino*. The collection would consume about forty minutes, and then he'd listen to a little Wagner. After that, some of Mozart's later quartets and violin sonatas, and by the time these were finished he'd be well into the night. He'd take his time soaking in the bath, then break out the beer and eat his deep-fried tofu and cabbage rolls. After dinner he'd listen to Brahms's *Hungarian Dances* and Strauss's *Metamorphosen*, and then, with two hours to bedtime, he'd allow himself some cognac and put on a Chopin nocturne. He had several – Ashkenazy, Rubinstein, Pollini, Horowitz – and he listened to one every night before going to bed. The piano always seemed to speak to him, saying, *Well, we've made it through another day. Time to think about turning in.*

He had a performance by Michelangeli that he hadn't listened to yet, and it was as he was thinking he'd check it out tonight that he first noticed something different about the atmosphere of the living-room. It was a vague sensation, as if he'd caught a faint whiff of some unforgettable fragrance, or heard a brief, barely noticeable ringing in his ears, or seen someone flit across the edge of his field of vision, or all three at once, and he leaned forwards on the sofa and looked around the room. 'Rie-san?' he said. It was her day off, but maybe she'd decided to drop by and fix dinner. She was genuinely worried about him, and it wouldn't be unlike her to do something like that.

'Rie-san?'

There was no answer. He sniffed at the air and looked towards the kitchen. Maybe something was burning. When he'd got up to go to the toilet a while ago, had he lit the stove to warm up the cabbage rolls? He'd been so unmindful and distracted lately that he wouldn't put it past himself to forget something like that. Leaning further forwards, he could see beyond the counter to the stove. None of the burners were lit. So what had just happened? He sat back and picked up the remote control to lower the volume on *The Sicilian Vespers*. One difference he was certain of: Gangsta was no longer barking, or making any other noise. Except when asleep, Gangsta was always either barking or scrabbling about, making his presence audible in one way or another – with his chain scraping across the edge of his doghouse, his tail flapping back and forth against his hindquarters, his hind leg thumping against the ground as he scratched himself, his footsteps pattering back and forth – but now there was only silence.

When he tried to call Gangsta's name he found that his vocal cords refused to vibrate or produce any sound, and that in fact he was having difficulty breathing. This discovery caused a sudden jolt of anxiety. He reached for the apple tea and took a sip, but he couldn't taste anything. Was something wrong with his sense of taste, too? Or had someone switched his cup? Maybe Shige had come home early, sneaked quietly into the house and decided to play a little trick on his old man, Aoyama was thinking, when a weird and spine-chilling sound split the silence. It was a sound like rusty hinges creaking, but he couldn't tell if it came from somewhere in the house or somewhere between his own ears. Everything went dark for a moment, and the sofa seemed to lift and then slam back down to the floor. And then, from the corner of the living-room, came a clear, succinct voice.

'Can't move, can you?'

When the curtains billowed and Yamasaki Asami emerged from behind them, he wondered if he was hallucinating. *Where have you been?* he tried to say, but the inside of his mouth was numb and no words came out.

She walked up to him and took hold of his face, squeezing his cheeks together with the thumb and index finger of her left hand. She was wearing rubber surgical gloves. The pressure of her grip was enough to force his mouth open, but he didn't feel any pain. All the strength had drained from his body, and it now seemed as if her one-handed grip was the only thing that kept him from sliding off the sofa. Drool was dribbling down his jaw. In her right hand she held a very thin plastic hypodermic. She showed it to him.

'Go to sleep for a while. I'll let you know when we're ready to start. Your body will be like a corpse, but I'll make sure your nerves are all wide awake. That way the pain will be a hundred times worse. So get some sleep while you can.'

She inserted the needle at the base of his tongue.

The liquid in the hypodermic seemed to saturate his body in no time. Aoyama did fall asleep, but for what seemed like only a moment. He was awakened by an excruciating pain in his eyeballs – as though they'd been speared from the inside with long pins that penetrated out through his pupils. His tears had a faintly medicinal smell. He couldn't move, couldn't so much as wiggle a finger, but certain sensations were extraordinarily vivid. He was able to work his jaw slightly, the feeling was back in his tongue and his sense of smell had returned. The tears misted his vision, and yet even the mist had a certain shining, crystal clarity. It was like peering through a fish-eye lens. Each time he blinked, he saw what looked like the after-image of a dead tree – probably the tiny capillaries on the retina itself – and heard something like the click of a camera shutter. Every little sound was amplified, and when Yamasaki Asami peered into his face and said 'Hello again', her voice reverberated like cathedral bells. His first reaction on realising that she was going to murder him was not, strangely enough, terror, but the sort of feeling of closure one has upon finally solving a puzzle. It hadn't just been a misunderstanding after all. It was about Shige. She hadn't been able to accept or forgive the fact that Aoyama had a son whom he adored.

Nor had Yamasaki Asami ever overcome, as Aoyama had believed, the trauma of being raised by a stepfather who beat and abused and reviled her. She still carried that trauma, still lived with it every day. Any man who betrayed or lied to her was the same as her stepfather; therefore, according to her reasoning, such men should have their feet severed to resemble him more closely. When not working at the part-time job that covered living expenses, she spent all her time preparing for the next operation. She would become intimate with a man and simultaneously begin forging a plan to cut off his feet should he prove to be just like her stepfather. In her teens, she'd only dreamed up the plans and never carried them out. She didn't have a proper tool, for one thing. It was while watching a cooking show on TV that she'd discovered the wire saw – a thin steel cable with teeth, and a ring attached

to either end. The TV chef had used it to cut effort-
lessly through a ham on the bone, saying that there
was simply no other tool to match it for this sort of
task. The wire saw had made everything possible. She
read up on pharmaceuticals as well, and found a way
to get her hands on whatever drugs she needed.
Thorazine, benzodiazepines, meprobamate, Valium,
medazepam, Librium, nitrous oxide, muscimole, am-
phetamines, psilocin, LSD. She had cased Aoyama's
home a number of times and even broken in before.
Having lurked outside since morning, she knew the
housekeeper hadn't shown up, and she'd seen Shige
leave with his skis. She'd slipped inside the house the
moment Aoyama stepped out to the market. On his
return he'd gone to the bathroom, and she'd taken that
opportunity to add a muscle relaxant to the honey and
yogurt mixture. If he hadn't made things that easy, she
would have been prepared to walk right up to him, say
hello and spray him with mace; but he would have
collapsed to the floor, and she much preferred having
him propped up on the sofa like this. It would facilitate
her work and make for a far more interesting picture.

She went outside and came back with Gangsta in her
arms. She plopped the dog down on the coffee-table,
between Aoyama's outstretched legs, and that was
when the terror kicked in. Gangsta was as limp-limbed
as a Beanie Baby, but at least that meant he was
probably still alive. Brushing the beagle hairs from

her black sweater, Yamasaki Asami went to the entry-way, where she'd placed a photographer's equipment bag. She took out a square black leather case, opened it by pressing on the corners, and pulled out something that looked almost like a portable headphones set – a thin, silvery, metallic cable wound in a circle, at either end of which was a ring the size of a large coin. She put her index finger through one of the rings and let go of the loop of cable. The glittering wire saw unwound with a sound like crossed swords. She wrapped the cable around the joint of Gangsta's hind leg, then took firm hold of both rings and looked up at Aoyama. Aside from the fact that she wasn't wearing make-up, her face was the same as ever. *Are you sure it's all right? I'm so glad. I've never had anyone I can discuss my problems with before. Can I really count on you to call?* Nothing in her expression distinguished her from the Yamasaki Asami who'd once said things like this to him. No psychotic gleam shone in her eyes, her hair wasn't standing on end, her mouth wasn't twisted in a maniacal grin.

She pulled the rings in opposite directions, as if stretching a chest-expander. There was a popping of ligaments and the awful sound of bone snapping, and Gangsta's leg became disconnected from the rest of him. The white fur of his stomach was instantaneously awash in red. Yamasaki Asami quietly extracted the saw and began winding it around Gangsta's other hind leg.

Aoyama tried to tell her to stop, but he had no voice. The Verdi overtures were still playing, at a low volume. *Aida*.

Stop it. He mouthed the words soundlessly.

'What's that?' she said. 'Did you say something?'

Not the dog, he tried to say. *Do me, not the dog*. And as he struggled to move his lips, he pictured Shige. Without a way to stop the bleeding, Aoyama knew he could die from an amputation like that. Then Shige would be truly alone. Shige was a good kid. The thought of making him suffer, of causing him any more pain, was unbearable.

He had to fight back somehow.

'The dog first, then you,' she said. 'Don't you want to watch him lose his head?'

Having finished wrapping the instrument around Gangsta's other leg, she pulled on the rings. The same awful sound. This time the blood splattered more, and some of it landed on the back of Aoyama's hand. Was there a way to stop this? If only someone would come. Not a salesman or delivery person, who would simply leave when no one answered the door, but someone who'd notice something amiss and investigate. If he could somehow toss one of Gangsta's severed legs out into the front yard, a passer-by might see it and . . . No. The two fur-covered objects lying there on the table were scarcely recognisable even to him. Anyone who'd never seen the severed leg of a dog might take it for a broken umbrella, or an odd-shaped handbag.

Maybe he could start a fire. If the house were burning, the fire department would come. But would they find him in time to save him? He couldn't walk, but maybe he could get to the floor, roll to the sliding glass doors and escape to the yard. No matches or lighters were at hand, however, and he wouldn't have been able to manipulate them anyway. The *Aida* overture was nearing the end. The next selection was *Masquerade Ball*, and then *Aroldo*. What if he raised the volume? With an awkward jerk of his arm he reached the remote control beside him on the sofa. Yamasaki Asami, winding the wire saw around Gangsta's neck, looked up at him. With unfeeling fingers he pressed the + key on the volume control, and when it reached maximum, he punched LOCK. Then, twisting to the left, he managed to force the remote control down between the back cushion and the springs. At full volume, the Bose speakers literally rattled the windows and caused the curtains to sway. Yamasaki Asami calmly stepped to the sofa and tried to retrieve the remote control, but it was wedged between the springs and she couldn't get it out even after flinging the cushion aside. Aoyama remembered that once, when Shige was blasting a Mr Children CD, a neighbour had rung up to complain. According to Shige the caller had been 'some old biddy' who'd threatened to call the police if he didn't turn it down. If only she'd ring up again and then, not getting an answer, call the police! Yamasaki Asami gave up on trying to extract the remote control and walked over to the audio rack beside the drinks cabinet. She seemed to be spewing some sort of abuse at him, but he couldn't hear her over the roar of the Berlin Philharmonic. She tried turning the volume dial on the amp and then pushing the STOP/OPEN button on the CD player, but with the remote control on LOCK none of the functions could be activated manually. The wall socket was behind the massive drinks cabinet, and there was no way to pull the plug. The music blasting through the living-room only heightened the unreality of the scene. A beagle with two severed limbs lay on the coffee-table in a pool of blood between the outstretched legs of a paralysed middle-aged man, while a beautiful young woman in a black sweater, jeans and sneakers moved about serenely in the background.

When Gangsta opened his eyes, Aoyama screamed – or tried to. His frozen vocal cords produced only a feeble squawk that not even he himself could hear over the thunderous music. The dog, whether because of the pain or because of whatever drug he'd been administered, was unable to bark or move, but his eyes said it all. They were the eyes of a creature gazing at its own death, a creature who'd been robbed of every last vestige of courage and dignity, and they filled Aoyama

183

with horror. Never before had he seen in any eyes, animal or human, such a look of utter despair.

Yamasaki Asami walked to the entryway and turned on the lights. Then she opened her equipment bag and took out a knife.

12

IT WASN'T A WEAPON, only a small penknife of the sort one might use to clean one's fingernails. The handle was pink, and the tip of the blade was rounded. There was nothing frantic or even hurried about Yamasaki Asami's movements, and her face was still a placid mask, as it had been even during the severing of Gangsta's legs.

She was looking for a place to cut the electrical cord. The amp and CD player and cassette deck were all combined in one unit that fit snugly into a custom-built shelf and couldn't be removed without disassembling the entire audio rack. The rack was flush against the side of the big drinks cabinet, and both were bolted to the wall at the back to prevent them from toppling in the event of an earthquake. She fetched Aoyama's fork from the coffee-table and inserted it in the narrow space beneath the amp, trying to snag the cord. If she could draw it out and cut it with her little knife, the music would stop, and his meagre rebellion would be quashed. He was going to die in the midst of this chaos and madness. It was too sudden, too soon, but maybe that was always true of death. It was probably best to resign himself after all, and to face the end with some measure of equanimity. Yamasaki Asami was still fishing for the cord. Even with the lights on, the narrow space beneath the amp was pitch dark, and she had to work purely by feel.

Aoyama had avoided looking at Gangsta since seeing him open his eyes, but now he realised with a gasp that the dog was dead. The light and lustre were quickly receding from those desolate eyes, and an astonishingly long grey tongue had slithered out from his open mouth. It was as if an enormous parasite were exiting the animal's corpse to seek another host. Aoyama wondered if the same would happen to him. He remembered reading somewhere that when prisoners were executed, their bowels and bladders emptied and their tongues hung out long and distended. He envisioned people looking down at his corpse, with his ankles severed, his tongue touching his chest, his trousers soiled, and the light gone from his eyes. It was a vision of astonishing clarity, as if he were actually witnessing the scene from somewhere outside himself: policemen milling about the room, a white-coated coroner examining his eyes, trying to judge the time of death by the degree of moisture remaining on them. Eyes that had lost the lustre of life, like the glass facsimiles on stuffed tigers or bears. Rie-san weeping into the skirt of her apron. Shige standing there numb with shock.

Where had this grim and vivid vision come from? He was thinking that it must be the drugs when he felt something explode in the pit of his stomach. It wasn't a nameable sensation like nausea or vertigo or heart-burn but an oppressive, violent sort of eruption. Whatever it was, it caused his blood to start circulating again, if only tentatively, and his legs began to tremble. It was as if something inside him were rebelling against the brain's command to surrender to death, refusing to give in.

He had to escape. He tried to flex the muscles of his legs, but they seemed to be disconnected from his brain. He had regained some control over his hands, however, and he clenched and unclenched his fists. Gradually the feeling began to return to his fingers. He could move his head as well. He hunched over and grabbed his right hand with his left, then lifted it and bent his head forward to bite the palm. He could feel the bite, but just barely. Yamasaki Asami turned to look at him, and he knew she'd finally snagged the electrical cord. He chewed furiously on his hand, biting down rhythmically, and was getting some feel-ing back all the way up his left arm. Just as he went to switch to his right palm there was a loud *pop*, the music stopped in mid-note, and all the lights went off.

Apparently Yamasaki Asami, slicing through the cord, had caused a short and triggered the breaker.

It was quite dark outside now, and even darker in here. Yamasaki Asami had melted into the shadows, but her voice came from right beside him.

'Where's the breaker? You ought to be able to talk by now. Where is it?'

Though she was close enough to reach out and touch, it was too dark for him to see more than the bare outlines of her face. But it was unmistakably the very face he'd once kissed and caressed, and dreamed of again and again. She might have been about to close her eyes and search for his mouth with her own. How many hundreds – no, *thousands* – of times had he pictured those features, so beautiful even when contorted in the throes of passion? For a moment he almost forgot about everything – his agony, his determination to escape – but the moment ended with a hard right hook to the side of his face. The punch was a shockingly powerful one, delivered with the fist that still gripped the fork. It wasn't as if she'd lashed out impulsively, compelled by some extreme emotion. It was, rather, a calm and methodical blow, intended only to reaffirm who was in control here. The tines of the fork had struck the corner of his mouth, splitting his lip. Blood ran down his chin, and the pain seemed to pierce his skull. Aoyama bent forwards and covered his head with both hands.

'The breaker,' she repeated, but without any inflection or affect in her voice. Obviously she hadn't the slightest compunction about inflicting injury and pain.

'Kitchen,' Aoyama said in what came out as barely more than a whisper. The breaker box was in fact built into the wall of a utility room next to the kitchen. In the darkness, it would take her some time to find the door and then to locate the box above the washing machine. Enough time, perhaps, for him to crawl up the stairs to the second floor, where the bedrooms were. Shige's room could be locked from inside, and had a telephone with a separate line.

Yamasaki Asami held the fork up for him to see, and then brought it down hard towards the coffee-table. Aoyama stiffened, but she wasn't aiming at his leg; the fork pierced the skin of Gangsta's neck with a nasty *squish*. The skin around the dead dog's neck was thick and loose, and the fork didn't penetrate far but dislodged and fell to the table the moment she let go.

As she disappeared into the kitchen, the pain in the left side of Aoyama's face reasserted itself. It felt as if he'd had a tooth pulled without anaesthetic. Blood from his split lip seeped into his mouth, and the warm, sticky taste of it weakened his will to fight. He could hear her walking around in the kitchen, the rubber soles of her sneakers squeaking on the floorboards. He turned his head to look over his shoulder and could just make out her silhouette, hands stretched before her as she groped her way through the kitchen. She moved cautiously, as if afraid of upsetting any dishes or glassware.

He used his hands to bend his legs, one at a time, and pull them on to the sofa beside him. Then he reached down to plant both palms on the floor and slide to the thick carpet. He managed to do this without making any significant noise. Using his hands and elbows, he began to crawl towards the stairs, and moments later he was out of breath. With the heater and ventilation system shut down, the dark room was weirdly silent. He stopped and tried to keep from panting by taking slow, deep breaths through his nose. He'd been able to vocalise the word 'kitchen' just now; maybe he should try shouting for help. From the houses next door came faint sounds – a television set on one side and someone playing a piano on the other. Even shouting at the top of his lungs once or twice was unlikely to bring anyone running – except for Yamasaki Asami, of course, who would make him pay dearly.

He dragged himself onwards. The sun had set completely now, and it was too dark to see the stairs, but he knew where they were. His forehead and armpits were wet with perspiration, though the room was cooling down quickly. He was beginning to get some feeling back in his toes, and he dug them into the carpet to help propel him forwards.

He had just reached the bottom of the stairs when he heard a sound and looked back to see the kitchen lit up with a bluish glow. *She's found the breaker*, he thought, and the sweat on his forehead seemed to freeze. But the light, he soon realised, was from a gas burner on the stove. She'd turned it on to provide illumination. Now she'd surely discover the door to the utility room.

He began his ascent. The steps were thick wooden planks, fitted into the wall at one end and bolted at the other to a fat steel pipe that slanted from the ceiling to the floor. There had originally been no railing, but at Ryoko's insistence they'd had one installed when Shige began toddling around on his own. The short banisters were threaded by a thick vinyl rope that served as a handrail. Aoyama rolled to his side and grabbed hold of the first banister with his right hand and the vinyl rope with his left. Pushing with his toes, he pulled himself up until he was sitting on the first step, then paused to catch his breath. He repeated the process with the next step, and the one after that. There were twelve steps in all, and facing the landing at the top was the door to Shige's room. Built in a sturdier era, the door was of solid hardwood. No woman could break it down with anything less than an axe or a sledgehammer. Aoyama had reached the fifth step and was trying to stifle the wheezing when he heard the door to the utility room click open.

Don't panic, he told himself. The utility room was cluttered and dark, and the breaker box was high up the wall. She probably wouldn't be able to reach it and would have to look for something to stand on. Aoyama banged his shin hard on the corner of the sixth step as he was raising himself up to the seventh, but he scarcely noticed the pain – more because of his own adrenaline than the drugs. His palms were perspiring, making it difficult to maintain a grip on the vinyl rope, and he kept wiping his hands on his shirt and trousers. Each little noise issuing from the kitchen caused his scrotum to contract. What sort of human being was this, he wondered. Piercing the base of his tongue with her hypodermic needle, severing the dog's legs with her saw, cutting the electrical cord with her little pink knife, slamming her fork into his face and then planting it in the dog's neck, all with the same expression she'd worn when brushing dog hairs from her sweater. You didn't normally strike someone unless in the grip of some powerful emotion. That's what violence was: emotion leaking out from consciousness into the physical world, linking up with the muscles of the arms and shoulders and diaphragm and, inevitably, the face. Stifle emotion during an act of violence and the face becomes a blank, unreadable mask.

Lifting himself from the seventh step to the eighth, he remembered something Yamasaki Asami had once told him.

When my real father died, my mother's new hus-
band came to the funeral in his wheelchair. I was five, I
guess, in kindergarten. At that age, you don't really
understand what death is – at least I didn't. I was
watching the priest, who was chanting sutras, and a
wasp flew down and buzzed around his head. The
priest was trying to shoo the wasp away and still keep
chanting, and it seemed so funny to me that I started to
laugh. And then I couldn't stop laughing. I bowed my
head and just kept giggling and giggling, and I guess
everyone thought I was having some sort of break-
down. But my mother's new husband was watching all
this. It wasn't long after that day that he hit me for the
first time. And I remember he was shouting at me as he
hit me, saying that anyone who could laugh out loud
at her own father's funeral wasn't even human. He
said it over and over, that I wasn't human, and kept
hitting me and hitting me . . .

Aoyama took hold of the tenth banister and pulled
himself up, pushing against the steps with his toes and
knees. Two more steps and he'd be on the landing. His
arms and shoulders were exhausted, but sensation was
returning to his legs, the blood beginning to surge
through them. He took hold of the eleventh banister
with his right hand and grabbed the vinyl rope with his
left. The door to Shige's room, painted a creamy white,
glowed softly in the darkness above him. There hadn't
been any sounds from the kitchen for some time now. I

might actually make it, he thought. And no sooner had he thought this than he heard Yamasaki Asami laugh. She was standing at the bottom of the stairs.

'So there you are!' she said. 'I'll be right back. Don't go away!'

Aoyama panicked. Two more stairs would bring him to the landing, but he was having trouble getting a good purchase on the step below with his trembling knees and bare, sweating feet. Lurching for the last length of vinyl rope, his hand slipped and he very nearly slid down the stairs. Shock and fear ballooned inside him, pushing all thought from his brain. It was as if he'd been dropped into the middle of a not unfamiliar nightmare: someone was chasing him and he could barely move. His arms and legs were only partially under his control, and negotiating the stairs was like trying to climb out of quicksand.

The lights came back on.

'I'll cut your feet off up there, then,' she said as she collected the wire saw from the coffee-table. She walked to the stairs and slowly started up.

No! Aoyama tried to shout. *No! No! No! No!* He couldn't even tell if his voice was audible. The balloon of fear was pushing with ever greater pressure against his temples, and when she touched his legs the balloon burst and the nightmare bled into reality.

'Turn this way a little. You want to see your feet come off, don't you?'

She wrapped the silvery metal cable around his left ankle, peered up into his eyes and pulled on the rings. The saw sank into the flesh and disappeared, and there was a loud *pop* as the Achilles tendon gave way. And the next moment, as if by magic, his foot, from the anklebone downwards, separated from his leg and fell to the step below. For an instant the bone showed white in the tendrilous cross-section of what had been his ankle, but then the blood seeped up and over-flowed.

'Look,' she said, pointing at the amputated foot and shaking the other. 'It's like a big red sea anemone, don't you think?'

Blood was gushing out of the stub of his left shin. It made a glubbering sound as it flooded over the side of the step and slopped to the carpet below. Aoyama was dumbly taking this in when, belatedly and all at once, the pain demanded his complete attention. He was immersed in pain, as if he'd fallen into a vat of the stuff. And then something mysterious happened. He was shaking his head violently, to stave off uncon-sciousness, when a strange silence filled the universe and he received a message:

Kick her.

She was squatting on the step below, wrapping the wire saw around his right ankle. Aoyama put his weight on his right foot and contracted his abdominal muscles to raise his left leg. She looked up, and he gave a grunt and poked her in the face with his bleeding stump. It was a pathetic, feeble kick, but it caught her right in the eye and was just enough to make her lose her balance. She let go of the wire saw and tried to grab the vinyl rope, but he thrust the stub in her face once more, connecting more solidly this time, with a sickening sort of *splat*. One eye daubed in red, she went over backwards, twisting as she fell. There was a thump as her head went down and her legs flew up, and another as she began a second somersault at the bottom of the stairs. The second one carried her over the carpet and ended when her back slammed against the wall. She sat there as limp and still as a discarded rag doll. Next to her was Aoyama's left foot, which had tumbled down the stairs behind her.

He wasn't sure how badly she was hurt, but he had other things to attend to. He was losing blood fast and slipping deeper into shock. Her right shoulder twitched and she tried to raise her head but then let it droop again. Aoyama hooked his elbow around the vinyl rope to steady himself. He was sitting on the ninth step, trembling so violently that his teeth were chattering. He squirmed out of his shirt and undershirt and pressed the latter against his bleeding stump. It was immediately saturated with blood, and he wrapped the shirt around it, securing it by tying the sleeves. He saw Yamasaki Asami place both hands on the floor, trying to rise to her knees, as he reached down to unwrap the wire saw from his right ankle. The saw was much heavier than it looked and inexplicably clean of any blood or gristle. He set it down beside him, then removed his belt and wrapped it around his leg, just below the knee, to make a tourniquet. He was too weak to pull the belt tight, so he fastened it and twisted the buckle until the leather bit deeply into his flesh.

As she tried to push herself up, Yamasaki Asami's right forearm bent in an unnatural way, and she stopped and slowly raised her head to peer at him. Her face was thickly smeared with his blood, and she was probably bleeding herself. She had struck the corner of a step with her shoulder and the edge of another with the back of her head. She managed to sit up, her broken right arm dangling. She lifted her left arm to wipe her face with the sleeve of her sweater, then gingerly touched the spot where her head had met the step. Aoyama was fighting unconsciousness by biting his lip as hard as he could and concentrating on keeping her in focus. There was no question of trying to drag himself up to the next step. She looked at him again and mumbled something he couldn't hear.

The doorbell rang. She flinched and turned towards the entryway, pulling a small canister from the hip pocket of her jeans as she did so. *Mace*, Aoyama was thinking, when the door opened.

'What the—?'

It was Shige. Yamasaki Asami staggered to her feet and moved towards him, holding the canister out in front of her, but tripped over her own equipment bag.

'Run, Shige!' Aoyama's attempt to shout came out as a choked gargle. Shige stood frozen, holding his skis and looking around him in bewilderment: his wounded father; the strange, bloodied woman lurching towards him; the remains of Gangsta on the coffee-table.

'Run!' Aoyama gurgled again, and Shige thrust his skis at Yamasaki Asami. She stumbled forwards and to the left, dodging the skis, and Shige spun around behind her. Aoyama was hoping that she'd continue on through the open door and flee, but she didn't. She pivoted to face Shige again and muttered something Aoyama couldn't make out. Shige dropped the skis and ran into the living-room. He looked down at Gangsta's corpse and up at his father, then shouted at the woman, 'Who the hell are you?'

She plodded after him, her right arm hanging at her side.

'Kill her!' Aoyama wheezed, to his own astonishment. 'Kill her, Shige! Kill her!'

Yamasaki Asami looked like a sleepwalker, or a zombie, plodding unsteadily after Shige with one arm raised before her. She squeezed the canister, but the spray shot off at an oblique angle and hung in the air of the living-room, the pungent smell of it wafting up even to where Aoyama sat crouched at the top of the stairs. She was still muttering, as if to herself. Shige ducked and spun towards the coffee-table to avoid the spray. He grabbed the glass yogurt container off the table, took a step towards the woman and hurled it in her face. It shattered against the bridge of her nose, splattering her face with white goo and leaving a gash between the eyebrows. Blood flowed from the gash and mixed with the yogurt, and she stopped dead in her tracks, still mumbling something. The violence of his own act seemed to paralyse Shige for a moment. Yamasaki Asami wiped her face with her sleeve, then raised her left hand and pressed the cap of the canister again. Shige jumped back and to the right, but a small amount of spray hit the left side of his face. 'Ow! Shit!' he cried, covering up with his hands and blundering towards the drinks cabinet.

Yamasaki Asami started after him, but suddenly came to a halt. Her lips were no longer moving, and her eyes had lost their focus. She put her hand to her head as she stood there, hunched and teetering. Now Shige was opening the bottom compartment of the drinks cabinet. He reached behind the wine bottles and emerged with the combat knife. Removing it from its hardened plastic sheath, he grasped the handle in his fist, blade down, and bounded towards her. She was still hunched over, holding her head, when he buried

199

the blade in the nape of her neck. Her knees buckled, and she crumpled to the carpet. Shige ran to the foot of the stairs.

'Who is she?' he said.

'Call police. And ambulance.'

'Right.' He turned to run for the phone.

'Shige. Wait.'

'Yeah?'

'She kept saying something.'

'Yeah.'

'What was she saying?'

' "Liar, liar" – just that one word, over and over.' Shige pressed the palm of his hand to his left eye and squinted up at him. 'What was this all about?'

Aoyama shook his head weakly.

'I don't know,' he said. 'Nothing, really.'

A NOTE ON THE TYPE

The text of this book is set in Linotype Sabon,
named after the type founder, Jacques Sabon. It was
designed by Jan Tschichold and jointly developed
by Linotype, Monotype and Stempel, in response
to a need for a typeface to be available in identical
form for mechanical hot metal composition
and hand composition using foundry type.

Tschichold based his design for Sabon roman on
a font engraved by Garamond, and Sabon italic
on a font by Granjon. It was first used in 1966 and
has proved an enduring modern classic.

ALSO AVAILABLE BY RYU MURAKAMI:

IN THE MISO SOUP

It's just before New Year, and Frank, an overweight American tourist, has hired Kenji to take him on a guided tour of Tokyo's nightlife. But Frank's behaviour is so odd that Kenji begins to entertain a horrible suspicion: his client may in fact have murderous desires. Although Kenji is far from innocent himself, he unwillingly descends with Frank into an inferno of evil, from which only his sixteen-year-old girlfriend, Jun, can possibly save him.

*

'Deft and fascinating ... A grisly tour of the darkness
and confusion of the human mind'
NEW YORK TIMES

'There is no shortage of terrors in this novel ... Atmosphere predominates,
and the claustrophobia of the backstreets of Tokyo is intensely imagined'
DAILY TELEGRAPH

'*In the Miso Soup* stays with the reader long after the book is finished and Murakami makes his readers as complicit as Kenji in their desire to understand why Frank is the way he is'
GUARDIAN

*

ISBN 9 780 7475 7888 8 · PAPERBACK · £6.99

BLOOMSBURY

PIERCING

Every night, Kawashima Masayuki creeps from his bed and watches over his baby girl's crib while his wife sleeps. But this is no ordinary domestic scene. He has an ice pick in his hand, and a barely controllable desire to use it. Deciding to confront his demons, Kawashima sets into motion a chain of events seeming to lead inexorably to murder...

*

'Equally compelling and disturbing ... a dark psycho-thriller'
DAILY MAIL

'*Piercing* is a Japanese extension of David Lynch's world: surreal, sexually anguished, highly neurotic, both knowing and naive'
GUARDIAN

'Each time a new book by Ryu Murakami is published, the people at the Japanese Tourist Board must hang their heads in despair ... Darkly witty'
DAILY TELEGRAPH

*

ISBN 9 780 7475 9313 3 · PAPERBACK · £7.99

ORDER YOUR COPY: BY PHONE +44 (0)1256 302 699; BY EMAIL: DIRECT@MACMILLAN.CO.UK
DELIVERY IS USUALLY 3–5 WORKING DAYS. FREE POSTAGE AND PACKAGING FOR ORDERS OVER £20.

ONLINE: WWW.BLOOMSBURY.COM/BOOKSHOP
PRICES AND AVAILABILITY SUBJECT TO CHANGE WITHOUT NOTICE.

WWW.BLOOMSBURY.COM/RYUMURAKAMI

B L O O M S B U R Y